MISS HILVERSHAM AND THE PESKY DUKE

SOFI LAPORTE

http://www.sofilaporte.com

sofi@sofilaporte.com

c/o Block Services
Stuttgarter Str. 106
70736 Fellbach, Germany

Editor: Shawnn Welde.
Proofreader: Stacey Ulferts.
Cover Art: Covers and Cupcakes.

ISBN: 978-3-9505190-6-8

❋ Created with Vellum

CHAPTER ONE

TO BE SOLD

*An excellent, well built, commodious mansion with a valuable
plot of garden ground including an apple orchard and a well of
Celtic origins, situated in Paradise Row and Chestnut Street.
For particulars apply to Bromley & Brown, Solicitors*

*M*iss Eleonore Hilversham was not amused.
The headmistress of the renowned
Seminary for Young Ladies in Bath looked up from her
letter and stared at the young woman who stood in front
of her desk. "Repeat that, if you please."

Miss Ellen Robinson balanced a stack of leather books
on her arm as she cast a worried look at her superior. "It
appears someone has moved into the house next door."

"You mean the Farraday home. The old couple finally
sold their mansion. That was to be expected." Miss

1

Hilversham stood up, stepped to the window, and lifted the curtain to peek out.

"No. The other one." Ellen lifted her chin at the window on the other side of the room. "The house with the wishing well. The one we intend to buy as an extension of our school."

Miss Hilversham shook her light-blonde head decisively. "You must be mistaken. The property is ours. We have an agreement with Mr Jones that the property goes to us."

Ellen carefully set the stack of books on the desk. "Then why does it appear as though someone just moved into the house? When my students and I returned from our walk this afternoon, I watched an Indian gentleman unload trunks and boxes from a carriage and carry them inside."

"Indian?" Miss Hilversham lifted a delicate eyebrow.

"He wore a turban." Ellen lifted her hands to indicate a turban shape around her head of copper-red locks. "He was young, handsome, and quite impressive looking." Her voice sounded dreamy. "He looked like a prince, but he was probably a domestic since he carried the luggage. But I wouldn't be surprised if he turned out to be a royal. He could've stepped out of *One Thousand and One Nights*. I read the French translation, you know, by Galland. And he looks exactly like—"

"Ellen!"

"Have you read the book? It is quite brilliant."

"I have, and I disagree. It is quite an improper book." Miss Hilversham looked at her severely. "Don't you dare read it with our students. It will give them all sorts of nonsensical ideas."

"Oh!" A pink flush covered Ellen's cheeks. "But the tale of Sinbad—I thought the children might—of–of course not." She cleared her throat and peeked down at her pile of books. When Miss Hilversham turned away, she unobtrusively turned the stack around so Miss Hilversham couldn't read the titles on the spines.

Miss Hilversham drummed her slim fingers on the tabletop. "As if this afternoon hasn't brought enough trouble: five ill students, an ill teacher, a choleric parent who doesn't understand he has to make an appointment before picking up his child, misdelivered packages, schoolbooks that are not arriving, a leaking roof, missing workers, and now a mysterious Indian prince occupying our house next door? What will be next?"

"I just thought you'd want to know, that is all. Also, we have moved the students out of the classroom with the dripping roof and into the library. We have set up buckets in the classroom, but some girls are making a sport of tipping them over, ruining the parquet. I will hound out the delinquents, never fear."

Miss Hilversham sighed. "Thank you, Ellen. I trust you are capable of handling everything. Just don't fall ill as well, if you please."

The woman flashed her a brief smile. "I shan't." She picked up her stack of books, which wobbled dangerously on her arm, and left the office.

Eleonore Hilversham took off her spectacles and rubbed her eyes. Ellen was a reliable, excellent teacher. She, as well as the other teachers, were more than just her employees; they were friends, family. But try as she might, she could not hold them. One after another, they left to marry. Hopefully, Ellen would stay on. It was so wearying to perpetually have to hunt for new staff. Miss Hilversham made a mental note to send another advertisement to *The Times*.

She looked through the window to the other property. Night had fallen. The dark outline of the neighbouring house peeked through the trees. It was as quiet and deserted as always.

Miss Hilversham had such big dreams. She wanted to unite the two properties and transform the adjacent house into a dormitory. Currently, the students both slept and studied here, and the building was bursting at its seams. With the new property, she would be able to build a bigger, better school. The two gardens combined formed half a park. They could build a lake, expand the lapidarium, and build a separate abode for the teachers.

But first, she would have to see that the damaged roof was fixed as quickly as possible. She knew it did not reflect well on her school that her students slept and studied under a leaky roof. She was teaching the daughters of dukes. They expected their scions to be housed properly.

The neighbouring property was to be hers soon. Mr Jones, the owner, had assured her repeatedly that she could sign the papers as soon as she had the necessary funds. After years of saving, writing solicitous letters to her patrons, and asking for donations, she had finally acquired the sum she needed. As far as she was concerned, it was her house. Her property. Her garden.

Eleonore sighed. It was getting late, and it was time for her to retire. Her eyes fell on a mahogany casket that stood on top of the commode. She lifted the lid, and, after some hesitation, took out the double floor. Inside was a little velvet pouch. She untied it and poured the contents into her hands. Her eyes clouded over.

There was a wishing well in the garden. She knew her students had made it a sport to visit the well at midnight, even though she'd strictly forbidden it. Several of her students swore it truly worked, claiming it to be responsible for their marriages to some of the most powerful noblemen in the country.

Eleonore was convinced it was all superstition, tosh, faradiddle and nonsense. No one in the possession of an enlightened, reasonable mind believed in wish fulfilment and, heaven forbid, wishing wells. Least of all a sensible, level-headed woman like herself.

That also pertained to love, of course. For Eleonore Hilversham did not believe in love. Aside from the fact that with her thirty-four years she had no prospects at all and was considered too old to get married, she had no desire to hand her hard-earned independence over to a man who'd considered her his property. It would never happen. For her students who secretly snuck into the garden to the wishing well to wish for a husband, she only had a slightly contemptuous smile.

But if it were true, assuming it worked…if she could make a wish, only one…she knew without a doubt what she would wish for.

Her fingers clenched over the pouch's content.

Her glance drifted over to the neighbour's garden again.

With a quick intake of breath, she made up her mind.

THE SUMMER NIGHT WAS FRESH, AND THE GRASS WAS WET. Eleonore shivered in her thin shawl and regretted that she hadn't pulled on something warmer.

Where did her students say they crawled into the garden? There ought to be a hole in the fence somewhere. She'd asked the gardener time and again to fix it, but her pupils always found a way through.

She lifted the lantern she'd brought along.

Ah. Here it was. How cleverly done! The thick boxwood fence looked impenetrable; however, when one looked closely, one could see that the cherry laurel that was planted right in front of it hid a hole big enough for a person to slip through.

Eleonore didn't think twice. She went down on her knees and shuffled through, taking the lantern with her. On the other side, she scrambled up and shook out her skirt. At least she now knew where the mud stains on her students' aprons came from. She lifted her lantern and looked about.

The neighbour's garden was more extensive than their entire school ground. Big and dark, the uninhabited mansion loomed in the background. The wind whispered through the trees, and the moon peeked forth from behind the clouds, casting a pale milky light over the garden. Eleonore couldn't help but shiver.

There was an apple orchard and a collection of birch trees off on the left. Behind those trees was the well. It did not look at all like a conventional well. Made of rectangular stone, it looked more like a pool, like a miniature version of the Roman baths in the city. Maybe once, it served some sort of function that only the Celts knew. She would love to have this well incorporated into her lapidarium. She had collected stone artefacts, works of art, and sculptures from the Roman times to create an outdoor classroom that both teachers and students enjoyed frequenting. This wishing well would crown it all.

She set the lantern on the well's edge, placed a hand on the stone, and leaned forward.

The water glittered black in its depths and reflected the full moon as it emerged from behind the clouds.

She recalled the words of her favourite student, Lucy, now Duchess of Ashmore. "You have to throw in a coin at midnight and say a wish with your eyes closed. And if the spirits of the Celtic well approve, they will collaborate to make that wish come true."

Eleonore snorted. It was all heathenish nonsense, of course.

But it was worth a try.

She pulled out the little velvet pouch, poured its contents into her palm and stared at it. The white moonlight made her hand appear ghostly white.

Emotion flooded through her. A pain so old, so deep, so fierce, it took her breath away.

She plopped in a coin and opened her lips to whisper her wish.

Then her head exploded in white-hot pain.

She saw stars.

Followed by a deep, dark, merciful blackness.

CHAPTER TWO

SITUATION VACANT

Exclusive private Seminary for Young Ladies in Bath is seeking a single, respectable, dependable, highly educated gentleman or gentlewoman for instructing Latin, history, and drawing. He or she has been expressly educated for this purpose and has the necessary references. Only serious contacts, please. Interested people apply to Miss Hilversham, Headmistress, Paradise Row.

*M*arcus Downing-Smith, Duke of Rochford, was in a foul mood.

He stared at the room in front of him with a scowl. There was no doubt this entire house was a hovel: the walls were mouldy, and the roof leaked. But this room was beyond anything he'd ever seen. There was a hole in the floor. Curse it if he hadn't almost stepped into it. He'd nearly fallen through and broken his neck, and then his proud dukely lineage, reaching back to the Norman times, would be forevermore extinct, snuffed out, gone.

The world, no doubt, would be better off without his sneering visage in it.

But he had lifted the candle and seen the dratted hole and jumped back, swearing.

He leaned over and peeked down. He could see all the way through to the dining room on the ground floor.

What the deuce had provoked Fariq to buy this hovel and induce him to live in it?

This damp, infernal, half-ruined shack in Bath.

His hand groped for his whiskey bottle before he remembered that he'd sworn off whiskey, brandy, wine, or any kind of alcohol from now till doomsday.

Only water and lemonade for him. And milk.

He swore again.

That's why he'd come here. Like an old, gout-ridden woman who came to Bath to partake of the waters to cure herself of her bodily ailments.

Except, it wasn't gout that ailed him. His ailments were so deep that no mineral waters could cure them, for certainly neither opium nor alcohol had been able to. Which was why he'd decided to be done with it once and for all.

He'd overcome his cursed opium habit. He'd gone to hell and back, and he'd nearly shattered in the process, but he'd done it. In comparison, this craving for a glass of whiskey was paltry. He hadn't been in his cups for a good several weeks already, and he was left in a perpetually foul mood, but he would get over this, too.

Admittedly, he couldn't have done it without his faithful former retainer and friend Fariq.

Fariq, who'd been by his side, caring for him every minute of his shivering and shaking, sweating, and swearing. He'd thrown every single Sevres vase he owned at the poor man, but Fariq had dodged them and remained by his side.

Fariq, the little scrawny street boy he'd picked up in Bombay, with the bright, inquisitive eyes, was now one of the most powerful men in London, filthy rich and the owner of his very own gambling den.

He didn't have to take care of his old master, but he did.

He didn't have to set out to purchase a house in Bath, so Marcus could stay hidden away in relative anonymity while recovering. But he did.

But what in hell's name had gone through the boy's mind buying this cursed half-ruin, right next to that school? What was it called again?

Miss Hilversham's Seminary for Young Ladies.

Bah.

It was the self-same school where his former ward had gone, once upon a time, before she ran away to London to find him. She was now in India, happily married to that blasted dandy, Viscount Alworth.

Not that Marcus wasn't happy that Pen had found her happiness; of course, he was happy for her. Except that Alworth, curse his soul, wasn't quite good enough for her, and that perpetually charming smile on the viscount's lips made him want to smash his fist into his grinning visage. But otherwise, it was all good, and they were all happy, he himself included. Happily ever after, and all that faradiddle.

Marcus growled.

What did Fariq think? That he'd be neighbours to his former ward's school, so he'd always be reminded of this infernal story?

He would pack up and leave as soon as morning broke. There was nothing here for him, and to Jupiter with taking the waters. He would be better off boarding a ship to India and getting a change of air. This wet, moist, foggy air here in England that clung to him like wet sheets did him no good. He needed the red-hot heat of India, the sizzling, scorching sun that would fry his brains and help him forget.

Though he suspected it would merely result in the opposite.

He pulled out a small keepsake from his breast pocket and stared at it moodily.

His thumb brushed over it. He swallowed and pocketed it again.

He'd have to inform Fariq about his decision immediately.

"Fariq!" Where the blazes was the man?

No answer.

Marcus eyed the hole in the ground with misgiving. Then he took a loose wooden board that leaned against the wall and covered it. It wasn't enough. The best thing was to cover it with something bigger—like that monstrosity that stood by the wall. He moved the dresser over the hole. Fariq would have to take care of it later. Or wait, maybe it wasn't necessary to take care of it at all if they were leaving first thing in the morning.

He heard the front door crash open.

"Sahib!"

Marcus frowned. Fariq only called him that when he

was distressed. There was an undercurrent of panic in his voice.

Marcus rushed down two stairs at a time, considering it a miracle it didn't collapse under his weight.

Fariq stood in the foyer, breathing heavily, barely holding up the burden in his arms.

Marcus saw two arms flopping toward the ground.

"Sahib, something terrible has happened. I killed a woman."

CHAPTER THREE

SITUATIONS VACANT

*Domestic servants wanted. A Cook. A Valet, A Butler, and a
House-Parlourmaid in a respectable gentleman's household.
Paradise Row and Chestnut Street. Apply to Fariq.*

She was back in her beloved Highwood again.

She skipped over the meadow towards her parents' mansion, twirling her sunshade. Her family was having breakfast outside on the verandah. Her younger brother was playing cricket in the meadow with the neighbour's children as they used to.

"The ball, Violetta, the ball!" Ned shrieked. The ball zoomed through the air towards her. She extended her lace-gloved hand and caught it. She'd always been good at cricket. Why wasn't she playing cricket anymore?

"Throw it back!" Ned cried, and she extended her arm to throw it across the meadow.

She couldn't throw it because she held something in her arm. A warm bundle that snuggled up to her. She dropped the ball and clung to the bundle with both hands.

A dimpled cherub's face framed with golden curls looked up at her.

Her heart widened, and she felt such happiness flush through her that she sobbed.

Then, from one minute to the next, the skies darkened, thunderclouds covered the skies, and the children abandoned their game and ran back to the house, shrieking.

Clinging to the child, she tried to follow them to the house, but she could no longer move; the harder she ran, the slower she proceeded. It was like wading through treacle. The bundle grew heavier and heavier. She was terrified of dropping it. She shielded it with her body, guarding it with her life.

Rain pelted down, and the wind tore at her skirts. She clung to the bundle, but then she held only an empty blanket.

It was always the same dream.

She moaned and thrashed about in distress.

"If she's not dead, she's definitely dying." The man's voice, a melodic tenor, was laced with a strain of panic.

"I don't think she's entirely dead yet, Fariq." The second voice was deeper, rather gravelly, and very masculine.

Little shivers ran down her spine.

"What happened?" the same voice asked. Someone prodded her arm. She wasn't lying on a meadow but something lumpier and more uncomfortable.

"I thought she was a robber, or something worse," the lighter voice replied. "I saw an ominous figure pass through the garden, so I took the poker and went outside to check who it was. It stopped in front of that wishing well, a sinister and ugly shadow. I was certain it was a robber or a *bhuta*, so I rapped the poker over its head."

"Turns out it's not a ghost after all," the other voice put in dryly. "But something worse. A woman. What the blazes was she doing there?"

"I suppose we can ask her once she awakes." There was a pause. "If she wakes." Another pause. "Do you think she'll wake?" A longer pause. "What do we do if she never wakes?"

This was awkward. She was in the presence of two men, complete strangers, who were poring over her prostrate body. Her mind worked feverishly. She could pretend to be dead a moment longer until, hopefully, a female servant came. For the moment, she decided this was the best course of action. It was, of course, an utterly ridiculous thing to do.

"She'll die." The younger voice moaned. "I'll be prosecuted, hung and thrown into Newgate for involuntary woman slaughter."

"The other way around."

"What?"

"Prosecuted, thrown into Newgate, and then hung. But since she's only a woman, with some luck, they'll merely transport you to Botany Bay."

"It's the same to me! I am done! Ruined! What will happen to my club?"

"Never worry about your club. In the worst case, I'll run your club. Easy, boy. She's not dead. Yet."

"You don't think so?"

"No, I don't. She just twitched her eyelid. Maybe pour

some water over her. Or what's that stuff women tend to sniff when they have the vapours?"

"Hartshorn salt. But I don't think we have any," the younger voice moaned.

"I only have my own snuff, which I don't share with anyone, especially not with prostrate women who wouldn't appreciate it. Special blend, you know."

"I don't think snuff is the thing anyhow, Marcus. I will try *Vishachikitsa* on her." The voice sounded grimly determined.

"Isn't that poison therapy for healing snake bites? That will really do her in if she isn't already gone. Besides, how is that supposed to help an unconscious person?"

"It's worth a try. It's the only thing I know. It could jolt her alive."

"I didn't know you knew this. When did you ever learn *Vishachikitsa?*"

"There are a lot of things you don't know about me." He sounded smug. "I picked up bits and pieces from our village healer. He was a very wise man."

"You can't have been more than a boy if that was before you met me, Fariq. Scrawny, hungry thing that you were. You tried to sell me snake ointment, and then when I refused, you tried to rob me. I remember the day very well. How long ago it was." The deep voice took on a softer tone as it reminisced.

"It was indeed. You threatened to thrash me and deliver me to the authorities unless I became your valet. Not much of a choice, if you ask me." Fariq sniffed.

"And yet you haven't regretted it one day," Marcus said affectionately.

Fariq sighed. "I have, by Kali's beard, I have."

"But think of all the adventures we've had together!"

Eleonore ground her teeth. So she was in the presence of a charlatan named Fariq, who dealt with quack snake medicine, and an immoral man called Marcus, who had no scruples to deliver his friend to the colonies so he could take over his lucrative club. It was all very good and interesting, but for how long were they going to wax nostalgic and continue exchanging their reminiscences? Her head throbbed and the back of her thigh itched. Her arm muscle was becoming cramped, and she craved a cup of good, hot tea. She clenched her fingers to wake up her arm.

The men fell suddenly silent.

"You know what I think, Marcus?" The younger man drawled.

"What, brat?"

"I think she's already under the sod."

"I agree. She's stone-dead."

"Dead as a mutton."

"A diet of worms."

"Pushing up the daisies."

Another pause.

"Marcus?"

"Hmm?"

"What do we do with the corpse?"

"Dashed nuisance." The deep voice paused. "Of course, we could always say we found her already dead in the house…."

"We could bury her in the backyard."

"Or drop her body in that well…"

"In fact, why don't we do that right now. Get rid of the evidence, so to speak."

"Right, let's do it. You take the left arm; I'll take the right."

She felt someone tug on her arm.

Eleonore shot up into a sitting position. "Don't you dare touch me!"

The two men pulled back, the slighter one with a surprised shout, the other with a slow grin spreading over his face. He was tall, with unruly black hair, and in shirt-sleeves. She'd never seen a more dishevelled man, nor a more handsome one, in a strangely depraved way. She had to remind herself not to gape.

In stark contrast, the other, younger man, clearly of Indian descent, was impeccably dressed in evening gear, complete with a turban. He was in his twenties and very good looking. No wonder Ellen had been so taken with him.

"Ah. Sleeping beauty decided to wake," the older man, whom she identified as Marcus, said. There was a challenging gleam in his eyes that rattled her. He'd known all along she was awake, confound it.

She winced as pain shot through her head. She placed her hand on the back. There was a bump. Instead of expressing any sign of solicitousness, fetching a doctor, or offering her a cup of tea, which would've improved her mood tremendously, the men merely stared at her as if she had sprouted daisies out of the top of her head.

She glared at them. "I see that neither of you has the manners of gentlemen, or else you would have already called a doctor and seen to my wound."

"Turn your head." Marcus gave it a perfunctory glance. "A mere bump. You'll live. No need to call the leech."

"I must say, I'm so glad you didn't drop your leaf,"

Fariq said with evident relief. "I was about to piss my pants, seeing myself boxed up in the louse house, or worse, packed off to lump the lighter."

"For heaven's sake. Must you butcher the English language so?" Eleonore couldn't help it. If her students ever talked like that, they'd be grounded for days.

Marcus narrowed his eyes. "If her ladyship's primary concerns are to complain about gentlemanly manners and refined language, she really can't be feeling all that unwell. What the deuce were you doing anyway, trespassing and stalking about in my garden in the middle of the night?"

"I beg your pardon?" Eleonore gave him her coldest look, the one she reserved for the naughtiest children. "Trespassing? *Your* garden? I must have misheard. This is my property."

The men exchanged startled looks.

"You must've hit her harder over the noodle than I thought," Marcus told Fariq and crossed his arms.

She glanced around, took in the half-furnished, dilapidated room, and frowned. "Where is this place? And who are you?"

The younger man stood to attention. "Fariq is my name." He bowed elegantly. "And this is His Grace, the Duke of Rochford."

Eleonore stared. "The Wicked Duke? Good heavens."

The man twitched up a corner of his lip and gave a crooked bow. "I see my infernal reputation has preceded me even to this remote corner of Bath."

She closed both eyes as her head exploded. "You are Miss Penelope Reid's former guardian."

Once more the two men exchanged glances.

"I am, indeed," the man drawled. "And who the devil are you that you would know my ward?"

"I am Miss Hilversham. The school's headmistress. Miss Reid was a former student of mine." She glared at him.

"Damnation," the man breathed.

CHAPTER FOUR

SEMINARY FOR YOUNG LADIES
Pleasantly situated, exclusive private Seminary for Young Ladies in Bath with Boarding and Day School opening enrolment to new students. Subjects taught: Literature, Latin, French, History, Geography, Arithmetic and Elegant Accomplishments. Only the best Masters with the highest morals and deportment are engaged. Peculiars may be known by applying to Miss Hilversham, Headmistress, Paradise Row.

arcus almost groaned out loud. She was the headmistress! Now here's a pickle.

The woman sat straighter than a rod of iron on the sofa, glaring ice-cold daggers at him. Fariq had almost done her in, and he couldn't blame him in the least. She was the haughtiest, coldest creature he'd ever encountered, with her odd colourless eyes and her light hair. Initially, he'd thought she was old, thinking her hair was

23

white, but on closer look, he could see it was merely a very light blonde. He stole a glance at her. How old could she be? It was impossible to tell. She could be anywhere from her mid-twenties to mid-fifties. He'd place a bet at mid-thirties. Around his age.

She had a smooth face with a narrow nose, a proud, high forehead, and thin lips that she had pinched together in disapproval. A younger version of himself would've been terrified, and no doubt that was the reason Fariq was fawning over her like she was the queen herself. She certainly had the bearing of a queen: proud and full of righteousness.

She made him feel like a schoolboy.

He disliked her immensely.

Nonetheless, he offered her a leaf. "So, you know Pen."

"You're the irresponsible guardian who neglected the poor child for years on end, not coming for a single visitation, ignoring all summons, ultimately causing her to run away to seek you out. I have heard all about you, Your Grace," she sniffed. "And the stories I have heard are not good." She had a way of over pronouncing words in a manner that raised his hackles.

Fariq grinned. "I wonder what kind of stories–" He broke off when he caught Marcus' glare. He lifted his hands in appeasement. "I will fetch you a glass of water, Madam. You look rather peaked around the mouth."

"Do that, Fariq." Marcus bared his teeth in an attempt to smile.

The woman kept staring at him. Surely, she couldn't have heard *all* the stories. She was a strait-laced schoolmistress in the far corner of Bath, so he supposed a little gambling and drinking would shock her horribly.

Although, of course, he was guilty of far, far more. Yes, he was a terrible, degenerate man, and in his case, the stories were all true. Alas. What did it signify?

And what did it matter what this woman thought of him? He never cared about anyone's opinion, did he? So why did he feel this sudden need to defend himself? Was this a blush creeping over his neck? Why did his hand creep up to his throat, wanting to loosen his cravat, to find nothing because he didn't wear one?

Ah, the woman was speaking again.

"Having clarified the point regarding your identity, where exactly am I?" She looked about.

"This is my house. And you were caught trespassing in my garden, which explains why Fariq had thought it expedient to whack something over your head. But no harm done, as I see your head is still intact. You ought not to skulk about in the middle of the night in other people's gardens. It is rather bad-mannered, which, as a teacher, you ought to know rather better than me."

If her eyes could shoot daggers, he'd be dead on the floor.

"This has nothing to do with being bad-mannered, as you put it, but with investigating a popular student haunt."

"Ah." Now that she mentioned it, he recalled his ward had told him that they'd liked to crawl through the fence to visit the wishing well in his garden. "But why the head-mistress would find it necessary to creep through that fence smack in the middle of the night to do the same begs some explanation."

A faint rose colour covered her cheeks. "I had to investigate what my students find so enticing here."

Investigate what her students were up to? Did she think him a greenhorn?

She evaded his sceptical look and continued, "As I mentioned earlier, this is my property, and I can do whatever I want on it. Even look at the wishing well at midnight."

"I imagined I'd heard you say something of the sort earlier. You belabour under a misapprehension. This isn't your property. I just bought it."

She shook her head firmly. "You are wrong. I am about to sign the contract with Mr Jones."

"He double-crossed you. Sold it to the higher bidder, which was me." He shrugged.

"Impossible. Mr Jones is a gentleman. He would never break his word."

"I can show you the deed."

"Please do." She leaned back, looking pale.

Fariq, who'd returned with a glass of water, left again to fetch the deed.

Marcus snuck glances at her. His ward had always talked affectionately about Miss Hilversham, but he could not, for the life of him, see the appeal. The woman was stubborn and stiffer than a board of wood.

He watched how she pursed her thin lips to take small sips from the water glass. Her fingers were long, slim, and white. She was clearly well-bred, a lady through and through; however, she was more of a schoolmistress than a woman. Schoolmistresses were oddly sexless creatures. Though this one seemed to have something about her that piqued his interest. He couldn't quite pinpoint what it was.

Fariq re-entered, bearing a document. "Here it is, madam. The deed."

She took the document and perused it, then lowered it with a distressed sound. "I seem to have lost my spectacles."

"Let me read it then." Fariq took the paper. "Deed. Made this fourteenth day in the year of the Lord eighteen hundred and twenty, between Mister Peter Jones, the first part, to His Grace the Duke of Rochford, M.D-S., the second part, for the consideration of etcetera etcetera paid in hand by the second party for the property, land and mansion, apple orchard and the wishing well, trees, yards, paths, etcetera etcetera in Paradise Row and Chestnut Street. The receipt thereof is acknowledged and signed in the office of Martin Brown and Peter Bromley, Queen Street, Bath, and recorded in Book 356 of Deeds page 243. The undersigned."

Miss Hilversham took the paper and squinted at it. She was silent for a moment as she placed her hand on her brow. "Bromley and Brown, you said?"

"Yes."

"It appears there must be a misunderstanding of the grossest sort."

"Misunderstanding?" Fariq patted the paper. "Excuse me madam, but it can't be any clearer. His Grace is the owner of these premises. It's black and white on here."

"I will contest it. This house and property were promised to our school, for a very long time, by the owner, and it was always clear I had first rights to it." There was a slight tremor in her voice.

"Too bad, because the gentleman evidently changed his mind and sold it to us." Fariq took the deed back. "I myself negotiated with him. He was very keen to sell it to us."

She narrowed her lips and lifted her chin. "Then it is unlawful."

The woman was clearly unhinged.

"Hogwash. You can apply yourself directly to the solicitors if you don't believe it." Marcus shrugged.

"And so I shall. What, may I ask, do you intend to do here? Surely a man like you would prefer to dwell in London?" She waved a pale hand. "To do whatever it is you normally do."

"Yes. All my wicked carousing and orgying." He gave her a feral grin.

She pulled her mouth into a distasteful line. "Pray, spare me the details, Your Grace."

Marcus studied her through narrowed eyes. A prude, was she? Concerned that his degenerate presence in this neighbourhood would despoil her innocent students? She didn't even need to put it in words, her entire being spoke of it. "We have grand plans for this house, indeed. Don't we, Fariq?" he heard himself say. He clasped his hands behind his back and rocked back and forth from heel to toe.

"Do we? I mean, of course, we do," Fariq added hastily.

"I shudder to think what those grand plans might encompass." The woman struggled up from the sofa. She was tall as she stood in front of him.

Those eyes! He'd never seen anything like them. He had to prevent himself from bending forward to inspect them. They shot slivers of ice-cold fury right at him. Hm. Fascinating.

Marcus crossed his arms. "Yes. Very grand plans. We'll

renovate it and set up, er, ah—a—ah," he snapped his fingers. "What did we say we'd set up here? Remind me, Fariq."

"Um. Er. A gambling club, Your Grace."

"Of course. There it is." He gestured grandly. "A gambling club, like the Perpignol in London."

"You would not dare!" she hissed. If he'd been somewhat younger, he would have been terrified. Fariq certainly paled.

"Oh, wouldn't I?" His lip curled. How far could he goad her? Could he make her lose her temper?

"A den of iniquity right next to my institution! We are a most respectable school, an exclusive institution for well-bred ladies of the country." She stuck her nose into the air.

Well-bred ladies! Ha! If there was a type of woman he despised, and mind you, there were not many—for he had a weakness for women of all shapes, sizes, and kinds—but if there was a kind of woman he disliked most heartily, it was a well-bred one.

Marcus grinned wickedly. "'Tis time the respectable breeding of those well-bred girls of yours gets a bit, ahem, expanded. My institution, for institution it shall be, will also be educational."

"Will it?" interjected Fariq with wide eyes.

"Oh yes. In our institution, people will learn all about the ins and outs of gambling." He made a bow to her. "I will send you an invitation to the opening. It will be *such* a pleasure to have you all here."

"I will not have it."

"Oh. Won't you?" He folded his arms across his chest.

"Mark my words, Your Grace. Do not underestimate me. I will not allow this."

"I wonder what you will do to prevent it. You are but a mere schoolmistress, and a priggish one at that."

She clenched her hands into fists, and he observed, fascinated, how her eyes formed to narrow slits of ice. "I will do everything in my power to prevent this."

He was enjoying himself tremendously. "Oh. Will you? I want to see that."

"And so you shall."

She nodded at them majestically and swept out of the house.

After she'd gone, Fariq looked at him with a troubled expression on his face. "Marcus. You didn't really mean that, did you?"

Marcus dusted off an imaginary speck on his sleeve. "Of course I did. Every word."

"In all seriousness? Are we to establish a gaming house here?" Fariq shook his head. "I meant it as a joke."

"It is no joke. I am deadly serious. It is a brilliant idea. It will take some investment. Let us start right away. We need to renovate this place and then set about planning how we build this gaming club. I want it to be even bigger, better, and more successful than the Perpignol. And you will be the head of it, of course."

Fariq shook his head. "By Kali's beard. If you ask me, the way you're reacting to her, it is as though you got whacked over the noodle, not her. Poor lady. Bromley & Brown have double-crossed her. Who listens to a mere schoolmistress when a duke who's plump in the pocket shows up and points his finger at what he wants? Add me into the bargain, for I do my job only too well when it comes to business negotiations. But I had no idea she had a previous claim on the property. Why not rent it to her? She's Pen's favourite teacher, after all. And I did nearly transport her to the afterlife. Let me pull some strings, and I'll get us something better on the other side of town in a jiffy. For one ought not to interfere with pale-eyed women of her sort. It'll only cause bad luck to rain down on our heads."

"You are wrong, Fariq. One ought to interfere, especially with pale-eyed women of her sort. I cannot stand the breed. Ha! I have found a new purpose in this humdrum life of mine, Fariq." He rubbed his hands. "We are staying here and making this our home. We are setting up a gambling den of the likes of which the world has not yet seen."

Fariq threw up his hands. "Anything you say, master." He threw him a mocking glance and left.

Marcus remained alone in the house with the slightly uneasy feeling that he'd just made himself a powerful enemy in Miss Hilversham. But that was balderdash, of course.

CHAPTER FIVE

NOTICE IS HEREBY GIVEN
that the private residence in Paradise Row and Chestnut Street
is not to be confused with the Seminary for Young Ladies that
happens to be located next to it. Direct your correspondences
accordingly. F.

Insufferable!   Insufferable!   Insufferable!
Insufferable!

Miss Hilversham, who was always in control of herself and trained not to reveal any anger, upset or anxiety, shook with passion. She stomped up the stairs to her porch, each step reverberating painfully in her head. When Martha opened the door, looking at her with great surprise, she snapped at the poor girl. "Bring me vervain tea, laudanum, and something cold to put on the back of my head."

"But what has happened, ma'am?"

"Just hustle and get me the things I need."

"Yes, ma'am." Martha hesitated.

"What's the matter?" She really ought not to vent her foul temper on the poor maid. The girl stood in front of her in a nightgown, clutching a candle and ogling her.

"It's just that I have never seen you without your spectacles before, ma'am."

Her hand went up to her nose. She'd already noticed her spectacles were gone at the house when she couldn't read the deed. Everything was blurred. She'd assumed it was from being hit on the back of her head, but of course, it must be because she'd lost her spectacles.

She froze as a realisation dawned on her. She'd not only lost her glasses but also the trinket she'd brought with her. It was precious. It was irreplaceable. It must have fallen out of her hand when she got clubbed over the head. A distressed moan escaped her. She collapsed into an armchair.

"Ma'am? Should I call a doctor?" Martha set down the candle and knelt next to her.

Eleonore grabbed her hand and patted it. "Yes. No. Oh, I don't know!" The pain at the back of her head was nothing compared to what her heart endured. She sighed heavily. "Do get me that cup of tea."

Martha nodded and left.

For one moment, Eleonore considered crawling back to the garden to find her trinket. Except it was night. She would have to grope around on the ground in the dark, and it was a nonsensical thing to do. She groaned. She would have to return the next morning. What a foolish thing to have done!

As she rethought the events of the night, fury swept

through her again. Who did he think he was? That awful, insufferable, detestable man. If she could, she'd be sorely tempted to swear, but she couldn't think of any satisfying swear word. She felt the headache take over her again.

Better not to think about it now.

Better not think about *him*.

Better just drink that tea and go to bed.

Tomorrow, she would feel better. She would be her usual, collected, firm self again, and she would come up with a solution, as she always did.

The next morning, she did indeed feel better. After a strong, bitter cup of black coffee with some toast, she felt her spirits return. Her head no longer throbbed, and she almost felt her usual self again. Thank goodness she had a second pair of spectacles, which she wore now, so the blurry vision was under control.

With that, her normal reasoning returned as well. She went to her cabinet and retrieved the file of Penelope Reid, her former pupil and student teacher. The poor child had been entirely unsuited for teaching and had been unhappy, pining for her guardian. Eleonore wrinkled her forehead. What on earth had Penelope seen in that terrible man?

She pulled out a document. There it was: proof. Marcus Downing-Smith, the Duke of Rochford, had indeed been her guardian. It was the same name.

Eleonore frowned. She realized that the man had been goading her. Gambling den, indeed! What utter nonsense was that? There were enough clubs in the city, no need to open another one here in the middle of a residential area. He must've said that just to provoke her.

But what was this about Bromley & Brown withdrawing their promise?

She sat down, penned a quick letter, and rang the bell.

Martha appeared summarily. "Martha, have this letter delivered instantly to Messrs Bromley & Brown. I require an immediate response."

"Yes ma'am."

There must have been a mix-up. A confusion. There would be a perfectly logical explanation. Bromley & Brown must've rented the house, which made sense, but the duke belaboured under the delusion that he'd bought it.

When Martha returned with the letter sometime later, Eleonore tore the letter open in the hallway.

Her hand shook.

Surely, she was misreading. She took her spectacles off, rubbed her eyes, cleaned the round lenses of her spectacles, and put them on again.

No, there it was, in black and white.

The property had indeed been sold at thrice the original price to the Duke of Rochford. It had been too great an offer to forgo. Mr Bromley sends his regrets, but Mr Jones had insisted on the sale. He offers another piece of property to Miss Hilversham as compensation. One by the river. It was somewhat smaller, but the price would be lower, too…

She snorted. It was a small, dingy property at the bottom of the hill where they lived, far away from the school and not at all suitable for her purposes. Mr Jones's greed had taken over, and he'd forgotten his promise to her. In this business, verbal promises counted for little when it came down to the promise of hard money, she thought bitterly. She had the funds for the amount originally agreed upon, but if the duke paid thrice the amount….that was beyond her means.

She looked up and saw Ellen descend the stairs.

"Ellen. Come here, please." She held out the letter. "Read."

Ellen read it and gasped. "This can't be true? So, I was right in my observations yesterday?"

"I am afraid so."

"What are we to do now? We counted on having the children moved to the other mansion so we could have this one repaired."

"That, dear Ellen, turns out to be moot, as from what I've seen, the other mansion is in even worse shape than this one. We cannot house the children in it at this point. Nonetheless, it is vexing that Jones, Bromley & Brown have broken faith with us in this ungentlemanly manner."

"You ought to have the Duke of Ashmore on the case. He's all-powerful. I am sure he could do something for us."

It certainly was an idea. She had three dukes, a viscount, and an earl to back her up as patrons. Surely, they would help her if she applied to them? Then Eleonore shook her head. "The Duke and Duchess are presently out of the country as they are touring the continent." She also felt that, for once, she ought to solve her own problems and not perpetually solicit other people for help. Even though they were her patrons, former students and friends, who were more than willing to help.

Somehow, there had been something in the face of the Duke of Rochford that had made all this rather…personal. What had he called her? A priggish schoolmistress.

She was a respectable headmistress, a strict but beloved teacher, an exacting employer, but certainly not a priggish schoolmistress!

"Ellen!"

The woman stopped on the stairs and turned to her with a questioning look.

"Before you are off to your next class....tell me something." Eleonore fiddled with the fringe of her shawl. "I am not....you wouldn't ever think...I mean..."

Ellen blinked, for surely, she'd never seen Miss Hilversham bumble and stammer in this manner.

"How to say this?" She cleared her throat. "One couldn't call me priggish, could one?"

Ellen's eyes grew to saucers. "Priggish? Oh no!"

Eleonore breathed a sigh of relief.

"Only..." Ellen hesitated, rubbing her hand on the rail of the stairway.

"Only what? Pray, speak what is on your mind, honestly and without compunction."

"You do tend to be somewhat...severe, in a strait-laced kind of manner. I don't mean this in a bad way." Ellen hurried to add as she saw something on Eleonore's face. "The Duke of Ashmore is also strait-laced."

"Strait-laced."

"Well, yes."

"You mean, starchy. Prim. In a sanctimonious, pharisaical kind of way."

"I wouldn't exactly say pharisaical but maybe...schoolmistressy."

"Schoolmistressy."

"Is this even a word? If you consider, all of us are schoolmistresses....so naturally, we'd be schoolmistressy, myself included." She broke off when she saw something on the headmistress' face.

"Indeed," Eleonore said coldly.

"I—I really ought to go see my pupils," poor Ellen stammered and fled.

Priggish schoolmistress! Something about the phrase disconcerted her.

It couldn't be helped. She had to visit her obnoxious neighbour again. She would have to sit down and reason with him, like the sensible adults they were. She hoped he would see sense eventually and sell her the property. And if not sell it, maybe rent it? Surely, they could compromise and come up with an amicable solution?

This time, she took the more conventional way through the front entrance.

She opened the iron gate, which creaked. She would have to have the entire fence replaced as the iron spikes on top looked loose and rusty, and if someone ever had the ingenious idea of climbing over it—she knew her students too well—they would find themselves impaled upon it. The fence had to go.

She walked along the pebbled path leading through the front yard up to the house. Naturally, the garden was in a disorderly state, not having been taken care of for years. The shrubs grew rampant, and the grass reached her knees. The garden was bigger and more generous than their own. When she removed the fence that separated the two gardens, it would be one grand, sweeping property. She could have a pavilion set up at the back near the wishing well for classes outside. If one cut away the shrubs on the side and replaced them with a smooth lawn, the children could play cricket there. There was even enough space for a pond. Eleonore stopped in front of the mansion and inspected it in the early morning light. The house was well constructed, somewhat older than the school, and in definite need of repair. The roof was possibly in worse shape than the school's, and one would have to replace the windows and shutters.

When she was done restoring the building, this house would be a beauty. She clasped her hands in front of her. How she could see it! It would be one of the most elegant, impressive schools in all of England.

Eleonore walked to the wishing well, scouring the ground for her spectacles and lost trinket. She found both lying next to the well, picked them up in relief, and dusted them with her fingers. She pressed a quick kiss on the trinket before pocketing it.

Then she squared her shoulders and turned to the house.

She raised her hand and lifted the knocker. It echoed hollowly inside.

No one came to open the door.

Now, that was odd. Had they moved out already?

She went to the window and peeked through the grey streaked windowpanes. There were no curtains, so she could see it was the same drawing room where she'd lain the night before. Aside from the sofa, there were trunks and suitcases, which meant the duke hadn't moved out.

She returned to the door and knocked again, this time harder.

Once more, she waited.

After knocking for a lengthier time, she decided no one was at home.

Turning to go, she heard a fumbling at the door, and the door finally opened.

"Pray, excuse the inconvenience—" she broke off with a gasp.

"The devil!" The duke glared at her. His black hair stuck in all directions, and he wore a pair of breeches that barely clung to his narrow hips.

And that was all he wore.

CHAPTER SIX

WANTED IMMEDIATELY

in select Young Ladies Seminary in Bath, a gentleman or
gentlewoman with a pleasant disposition and good address,
sound knowledge and competence to instruct Music. Respectable
references required. Letters, post-paid, to Miss Hilversham at
Paradise Row.

*E*leonore opened and closed her mouth like a startled donkey, and she may have uttered a similar sound as well.

He was quite glorious. Like that Greek statue of massive muscular masculinity she'd seen in the British Museum a while ago. Poseidon or Hercules. Or had it been Hades? Her frazzled mind could not recall the details. At any rate, the Duke of Rochford must have stood as the model. His shoulders were wide and powerful, of an even bronze colour, and there were tufts of fine black hair on his otherwise smooth chest.

Eleonore swallowed, tore her eyes away and fixed her stare intently on an obscure point behind him.

"What are you doing here?" he growled, placing his hands at his hips as if he were entirely unaware of his state of undress.

Eleonore folded her arms across her chest. "Pray, cover yourself. This isn't seemly."

A slow, feral smile spread over his face. "Forgot. You're a priggish schoolmistress, yes?"

There it was again, that phrase. He used it to goad her deliberately. A flash of temper flared through her and remained sizzling at the bottom of her stomach. "This has nothing to do with me being a schoolmistress, priggish or otherwise, but everything with you lacking any sort of good form or breeding of gentility and refinement as befits a gentleman of your class."

"You labour under a misapprehension, lady. Surely you must've heard that I am neither in possession of gentility nor refinement. And I couldn't care a tuppence about any gentlemanly behaviour. As you so aptly pointed out yesterday, they call me The Wicked Duke. I try my best to live up to that name." As he stalked back inside, he hitched up his pants, leaving her standing in the open doorway, thoroughly put out.

It took Eleonore a while to collect her wits. She pulled herself up, took a big breath, stepped into the house, and closed the door. Now, in the light of day, she could see the state of the house. There was hardly any furniture, save for the threadbare sofa in the drawing room, whose acquaintance she'd already made the night before. On the floors, bare of any carpets, were half-opened trunks and suitcases spilling out with clothes, books, and what appeared to be exotic art. Dust motes floated about in the sunlight, pouring through the uncovered, streaky windows, tickling her nose. She repressed a sneeze. Cobwebs hung from the ceiling like scraps of wispy lace from a long-forgotten era. If she were to drape her gloved finger over the top of the doorframe, it would come away stained with a thick layer of grey dust.

The duke was in the drawing room, rummaging about in the trunks. He took out a scarlet, silken banyan, hopelessly rumpled yet delicately embroidered with intricate oriental patterns. He put it on but left it hanging open. It draped behind him like a mantle as he walked from trunk to trunk, searching for something, muttering. He looked glorious in it, like a degenerate, exotic kind of king. His dark, thick hair contrasted with the deep red.

The man badly needed a haircut. The thought shot through Eleonore's distracted mind, and she wondered what it would feel like to pull her fingers through his thick mane.

Shocked by her thoughts, she took a step back and bumped into something. It was a white porcelain elephant, tall enough to reach her knees, with a flat surface on top, but it was not big enough to serve as a table. It wobbled dangerously. She reached out to secure it before it toppled over. Most items standing about randomly seemed to be oriental art, vases, and statues.

She picked up a tapestry that lay half-unrolled by her feet. It was a bright turquoise-blue peacock, with little mirrors sewn into it. She'd never seen anything so beautiful before. "Is this Indian?"

The duke turned. "What, you're still here? I thought you'd be over the hills of Bath by now, having seen me in my indecent, half-naked glory. And yes, this is Indian. Put it down before you drop it. It's valuable."

She rolled it carefully and set it down on top of a delicately carved side table that also seemed to have been brought from India. The duke seemed to have exquisite taste in art. She found that difficult to reconcile with his otherwise coarse, boorish behaviour.

"Why are you here at this ungodly hour? Your hammering would have woken the dead. I haven't even had breakfast yet."

"It is," she flipped her pocket watch open, "a quarter before noon. Hardly ungodly. The greater part of hard-working mankind has been up and about for half the day already. But of course, that wouldn't apply to Your Grace, your kind not being used to doing any sort of honest work." She pulled her lips down sarcastically.

"You are certainly right about that." He pulled his hand through his thick mane and looked about with a distracted air. "Where the deuce is Fariq?"

"If you mean the man who attacked me last night, I do not know where your servant is. I am still awaiting an apology from him." The duke hadn't even asked how she was feeling, nor whether the lump at the back of her head was still hurting. She glowered at him.

"Fariq isn't a servant. You will have to wait for a long time for an apology, lady. He only did what any man in his right mind would've done. He defended my property. You shouldn't have been skulking around here in the middle of the night."

Eleonore took a big breath, counted to three, and then exhaled slowly. He was goading her on purpose. She had to keep her temper in check if she was to achieve what she came for.

She put up a frosty smile. "This is precisely what I have come to discuss. I have been corresponding with Bromley & Brown, and they have confirmed the—in my opinion—precipitous and actionable transfer of this property. It has been understood all these years that our school had first claim on it; so, you may understand my astonishment regarding the revelation that the solicitors have not been dependable in their business."

The duke continued to rummage about in another trunk. Aside from a grunt, he did not indicate that he'd heard her. She followed him to an adjoining sitting room, where he fiddled around with the lock on a suitcase. "I have therefore come to the monumental decision that I have to take matters into my own hands."

"Speaking of hands, hold this, will you?" He fished a statue out of the trunk and handed it to her. Eleonore took it, taken aback. It was a bronze figure of a naked woman with six arms. "But don't drop it."

Pushing her spectacles up her nose, she turned it and inspected it. "It is the Goddess Kali, yes?"

"Behold me astonished. The schoolmistress is capable of identifying a heathenish statue. Ah, here it is." He pulled out something that looked like a pipe. He wiped it on his breeches, stuck it into the mouth and looked about for something to light it.

"Stop calling me schoolmistress. And why wouldn't I

know what it is?" She set the statue down carefully. "But you are deflecting. I haven't come here to discuss Kali, but the business at hand."

"I haven't even had breakfast yet, and you expect me to discuss business on an empty stomach?"

"Indeed."

He seemed to debate with himself. "Very well, come with me."

Relieved that he finally seemed to see reason, she followed him down the hallway, a flight of stairs, along another narrow hallway, but instead of into a study or library, as she expected, he led her to the kitchen. It was a big room with a massive table in the middle, a stove on the side, and various rusty pots and pans hanging on the walls. The kitchen hadn't been used in years, and one could see that. Goodness, the place needed to be thoroughly renovated before her children could move in here. It was going to be a tremendous amount of work.

"Sit," the duke pointed to a rickety chair. He took the pipe out of his mouth and placed it on the table.

She sat at the edge of the chair, expecting it to collapse any minute.

He busied himself pouring water into a kettle and making a fire in the stove.

Eleonore watched for a while, too astonished to find words. The Duke of Rochford was putting a hand to prepare his own breakfast? She knew he was outlandish, but that was beyond anything she could have imagined.

"Don't you have a cook?" she blurted out.

"No. Fariq cooks, but he isn't here, and I need my breakfast." He turned to her, holding a small copper saucepan in his hand. "Do you want some masala chai?"

Eleonore thought quickly. She had no desire for masala chai, whatever that was, but if it bought her some time to negotiate with the difficult man, then so be it. "If you please."

She watched him fiddle around with the saucepan, add some spices to the water, and after a while, an aromatic, spicy scent filled the air, which made her mouth water. He poured the liquid into a mug and handed it to her.

It was a brownish, milky liquid that smelled of cinnamon, cloves, and something spicy. She sniffed at it suspiciously.

"It's not poison. Go on. Try it."

She took a tentative sip. Her mouth exploded in an amalgam of aromatic sensations. She'd never had anything so good before.

"Do you always cook for yourself when your servants aren't here?" she asked.

"Yes." He looked about, and in the absence of a second chair, grabbed a wooden box, turned it vertically and sat on it. "I'd rather cook for myself than eat the tasteless pap of English cooks. Force of habit. When you have to survive two wars and a fortnight alone in the jungle, you learn not to depend on your butler, valet and cook, especially after they've been blown to smithereens." He stared moodily into his tea. "Blasted Maratha war."

Eleonore clasped a hand over her mouth.

"I've been able to fend for myself and to take care of my own needs since I was a child. My father insisted on it. So, you see, my kind is capable of some honest work, after all."

How astonishing they were having a perfectly civilised conversation. It was interesting, too. She felt prompted to ask about those wars and excursions into the jungle, and what an extraordinary man his father must have been if, as a duke, he'd insisted his offspring learn to see to his own needs but restrained herself from asking. As fascinating as he was, and as much as she felt tempted to inquire further, it was better not to get too intimate with one's opponent. For opponents they were, no doubt about that.

"I wanted to talk about business." She set down her cup with a clank, pushed up her spectacles, and pursed her lips.

"Ah yes. Business." He lit his pipe, popped it into his mouth, and lifted a regal hand. "Proceed." The rich smell of tobacco suffused the air. It was familiar, it was homely. Her father, too, had smoked a pipe. How long it had been since she'd last smelled this.

She swallowed the lump in her throat. "To tie in with what has been said previously, Bromley and Brown have offered me property in lieu of this one. It is of similar size, in an excellent location, near the river, right in town. My proposition is a transaction in which both of us benefit."

"Transaction?" He lifted an eyebrow as he kept puffing away on his pipe.

"A commutation, of course."

"Am not following," he growled. "My mind is too simple-minded for your advanced academic vocabulary."

"A trade?"

"Trade? As in swap?"

"Precisely. I see you have understood the nature of my proposal. You, instead, take the property Bromley offered to me, and leave us—meaning the school—this one. Surely you have no particular personal attachment to the house

50

and property here? Other than wanting to transform it into a gaming hell, I mean."

He seemed to ponder her suggestion. "Not particularly."

"Excellent. So, there is nothing in the way of—"

"But then who knows where that other property is?" he mused. "Might be damp, or prone to flooding if it's close to the river."

"In the city. Closer to your clubs and the general hubbub of social life that no doubt you're a part of. You will be welcome to open your club there; in fact, it would be the perfect location. Not here," she lifted a slim, white hand, "in the middle of a respectable, quiet residential area. You will meet with fierce resistance. Surely you see the reason behind that?"

He shook his head back and forth. "But I have come here to seek solitude, so why trade that off for something in the hustle and bustle of town?"

"Surely you can see the advantages. Man of the world that you are. Why hide yourself away here?"

"Because that is what I intend to do? To live here in peace and quiet?"

That took her aback. "Really? That makes no sense. You wanted to open a gaming club, if I may gently remind you. That is incompatible with the peace and quiet you claim to seek."

"Ultimately, I came here to take the waters like everyone else. The club is a beneficial side business. It will operate only at night. Fariq is already working on it."

She huffed. "Then at least think of the school children. It would be for their benefit. Your ward, as you very well know, attended this school. Isn't that reason enough to have a more charitable frame of mind?"

He scratched his head. "I don't know. Is it?"

Insufferable man! She was quickly losing patience with him. She ground her teeth. Patience! "Well?"

"Fact of the matter, ma'am, is that I trust in Fariq's estimation, and he had good reason to choose to invest in this property for me. If he says it's the best in Bath, then the best it is, and that is that. I don't give away what I already own. What's mine stays mine. I won't ever give anything away to charity, not to a bunch of school-children, and certainly not to you."

"Is this to be your last word?"

"It is."

"Then there is no reason for me to linger here."

"No. No reason at all." He gave her a sinister smile.

Eleonore stood up, and the chair toppled over with a crash.

Suddenly, she was aware that she was alone with him in this room, in the entire house, that he was only half-dressed, and that she was feeling altogether too hot in her skin. She did not like the decadent look on his face, his half-closed eyes as he assessed her figure; and the memories of his reputation and all the stories and the women he ruined rushed back to her. They said he had had more women than a sultan in his harem.

It had been unwise to come here.

"Thank you for the tea." She backed off. "I shall see myself out."

He got up and towered over her.

She turned and tore the door open, rushed through, and found herself sprawled on the floor between buckets, mops and brooms, shoe polish, silver polish, bars of carbolic soap and borax powder, which had toppled from the shelf above and scattered all over her.

She sneezed.

The duke slapped himself on his thigh and roared.

Really. He had the infantile humour of a silly schoolboy.

She glared at him as she pushed aside the mop that had fallen over her head, scrambled up and dusted the borax off.

"Wrong door. In case you haven't noticed," the duke managed to say eventually.

"I noticed, thank you very much," she ground out between gritted teeth.

"You, um, still have something." He gestured with his hand and grinned.

She glowered at him.

"Here." He stepped closer, raised his hand, and suddenly she had a straight view of his chest. She smelled a very masculine smell of cinnamon, tobacco, and musk. He lifted his hand, and she shrank back. He picked off something from her head and showed it to her. A dust rag. "You also have some white stuff." He gestured at his head but broke off when he noticed the deadliness in her eyes. "Never mind."

Terrible man! How dare he be so amused at her mishap?

"The exit is over there." He pointed at the door next to the storage room.

With a huff, she returned to the seminary.

When Martha opened the door, she gasped. "Ma'am! What happened?"

"I had an accident." Eleonore spied a vision of herself in the mirror in the hallway and froze. She looked like a ghost.

She'd clearly lost this round. She had to retreat and think of the next step. For she would not give up. Never.

CHAPTER SEVEN

WANTED

Miss Hilversham's Seminary for Young Ladies urgently seeking a roofer, mason, plasterer and carpenter for immediate employment, Paradise Row 24, not 26. (That is, to repeat: Twenty-four, NOT Twenty-six). Miss H.

"I don't understand it," Eleonore said to Ellen, who was sitting at a desk in the library, bending over a pile of student papers. The sun shone through the library windows and lit up reddish streaks in her auburn hair. "It is the second week in a row that I am placing an advert for workers and craftsmen, and not a single one has come. It is most unusual. Especially since I know that there are workmen seeking employment. I even sent Martha directly to the local roofer, and he assured us he'd send us his men imminently. Why didn't anyone come?"

Ellen placed down the quill. "You are right. There hasn't been a single worker showing himself. I fear—" she bit her lip.

"Speak your mind, Ellen." Eleonore massaged her temples.

"I fear that our ignominious neighbour may be at fault."

Eleonore dropped her hands. "What do you mean?"

Ellen got up and drew the curtain aside. "They don't seem to have any problem whatsoever finding workmen. Don't you think that is odd?"

"Odd?"

Eleonore stepped to the window and looked outside. Indeed, there was the sound of hammering, and when she looked closely, there were two, no, three men on the roof, busily hammering away.

"Odd that they seem to be able to hire roofers with no problems, whereas we...."

"There is nothing odd about it whatsoever. It is a malicious plot!" Eleonore dropped the curtain.

Ellen widened her eyes. "But that is a little out of the way, don't you think?"

Eleonore shook her head decisively. "I have talked to him. I attempted to reason with him. I even offered him a trade. But the duke will have none of it. On the contrary. He has made it clear that he will do anything in his power to vex us."

"What on earth have you done to incur such a wrath in him?"

"I have no idea, Ellen." Eleonore dropped into her chair with a sigh. "The man has taken an intense dislike to me. If I say one thing, he will say the opposite just to infuriate me. I was rather certain at one point he had no interest in the property; in fact, he hadn't even settled in yet. I could have sworn he might have left. That he hasn't may be entirely my fault. If I'd shown less of an interest, he might well have left the matter alone and returned to London, pursuing whatever he normally pursues. But now he is fixated on installing a gambling club in there." A look of distaste crossed her face.

"He is most definitely restoring the house. At breathtaking speed, too. Their roof will be mended by the evening, whereas ours…"

Martha came into the room. "Ma'am, there is a delivery. It seems like the furniture has finally arrived. Except, it's somewhat odd."

"Odd? What do you mean?" Eleonore puckered her forehead.

Martha gestured helplessly with her hands. "Come see for yourself."

In front of the school stood a cart from which two men unloaded bulky furniture.

Except for the expected new school desks, chairs, and chalkboard, it was a table of some sort, of gigantic proportion.

"What is this?" Eleonore pulled aside the drape that covered one of the tables and revealed a green baize stretching over its surface.

A man with a cap ticked off the order on a sheet of paper. "One billiard table, two faro tables, eight leather armchairs. Where do we put them?"

Two men unloaded the tables and looked at her expectantly.

"This must be a mista—" Ellen started.

"Quite right. The billiard table in the library, and one faro table each in the drawing rooms, if you please." Eleonore stepped aside to let the men pass.

Ellen shut her mouth with an audible snap. "But this is clearly a mistake?" she whispered.

"Just play along." Eleonore walked ahead to tell Martha to open the double door.

The men delivered the furniture to the respective rooms.

Eleonore signed the paper.

The men tipped their hats and left.

"Miss Hilversham. Do you care to explain what we are to do with faro tables in the drawing rooms?" Ellen looked at the offensive tables with mistrust.

"Use your imagination, Ellen. You're a talented teacher. I'm certain you can come up with something."

"But—we as good as stole their furniture."

"It must appear like that. In fact, it was a mistake, was it not? Keep in mind what the purpose is. Without a faro table, they won't have a gaming club. As simple as that."

Ellen bit her lip. "I admit it is rather worrisome that they would open a gambling hell right next door to our school. I never thought it possible."

"Neither did I. Rest assured, I will have the entire parish on this case. His Grace will not have a moment's peace. Plus, he will never know what happened to his furniture." She smiled thinly.

"I've never known you to be this quarrelsome," Ellen said pensively.

"This is war, Ellen. I want that property for our school. I will not have it turned into a den of sin and vice."

"And what about this?" Ellen lifted a wooden board. "I found it just now attached to our fence."

There was a big, red arrow on the board, and the words: "All workers to nr 26."

"What is this?"

"The explanation why no worker ever rang at our door. They went straight to our neighbour. You were right. It is a malicious plot."

"The audacity!" Eleonore hissed. "He's taken our roofers literally from under our noses! I see I will have to talk to our inglorious neighbour once more. Except this time, I will not suggest a polite trade."

"Do be careful. I have heard such stories about the duke. He's not one to be trifled with."

"Don't worry. He is but a man. And men want to be controlled. That is all."

Eleonore marched over to the duke's house.

She rapped loudly on the door.

A young footman opened the door. "Yes?" He looked at Eleonore cluelessly. It looked like the duke had even been successful in hiring new domestics, whereas they had not. It was beyond the pale.

"One commonly receives a guest with the words, 'How may I help you, ma'am?'"

"Oh no. It's Miss Princum Prancum. What does she want now?" a voice bellowed from inside.

"My name is Miss Hilversham," she informed the footman with cool tones. "Do inform His Overbearing Grace, who, I gather, has deigned to rouse himself from sleep already, that the headmistress of the seminary for young ladies next door is requesting a parley. Imminently."

"Requesting a—what?"

"A par-ley. It is a conference of two opposing parties to discuss terms. You had better learn expressions like this quickly if you are to be the footman of a duke."

That merely earned her another blank stare.

"Tell Miss Princum Prancum that the duke has no time for poppycock and palavers," the voice boomed from inside.

"Pala—?" The footman lifted a helpless hand.

"Tell his august dukeship that it would be in his best interest to comply with a parley. And that he will regret it deeply if he does not concede." Eleonore hissed.

The poor footman merely stared at her unhappily.

The door flung open as the duke stepped forward. "She thinks we're at war, you see." With a jerk of his head, he sent the footman away. "I'm not inclined towards having any parleys. According to my understanding of the definition, a parley includes the negotiation of an armistice. Which I am prone to decline. What do you want?"

Once more he was half-dressed, but at least he was wearing a shirt and trousers under his banyan. She felt the itch to tuck in his shirt and pull up his trousers.

"An explanation for this." Eleonore pushed the wooden board forward.

He tilted his head sideways as he read what was on it. A grin spread over his face. "Must've been Fariq. Clever of him."

"Clever? What about our workmen? We advertised first. You have stolen them from right under our noses!"

He shrugged. "Bad luck if they came to us first.

Besides, you shouldn't be saying anything when your party was the one who started this to begin with."

"I have no idea what you are talking about."

He took the board and turned it around. On it, in childish letters, was written: "This is our pruperty."

"What is this?"

"You, madam, need to control your children better. Fariq found this attached to my gate the other day." He pushed his face forward. "Some might say this is a declaration of war."

His eyes were green. A sparkling, clear, emerald green, with little mischievous orange specks in them. They were mesmerising. She felt a tug of attraction and recoiled.

Puckering up and summoning her stiffest demeanour, she retorted, "They were no doubt provoked to post this sign out of fear of losing their educational future," she said. "It is entirely understandable."

He studied the sign again and shook his head. "Their spelling ability is not exactly a recommendation of your teaching quality, is it? 'Pruperty'. Really? Tsk."

Now he was insulting her teachers? How dare he? "We have the best teachers in the kingdom," she hissed. "And our education is one of the best in the country. So don't you dare insult my teachers."

"My, my, someone seems to have thin skin. It's turning rather red, too. Touched a nerve, have I?"

Her hand involuntarily crawled up to her neck. She did feel rather hot.

"And now her eyes are shooting darts of silver ice at me again," he mused. "When you narrow them like that, behind those awful spectacles of yours, you look rather intimidating." He uttered a sudden laugh. "Like a cat that's about to spit at me, sheathing her claws. Do you have claws as well, Miss Puss?" He laughed again. "I daresay you do."

"I bid you good afternoon, Your Grace," she said frostily and turned on her heel.

"Is it afternoon already? Could've sworn it's only morning. By the by, Miss Puss."

"The name is Hilversham," she hissed.

"Whatever. Tell your students to refrain from practising their singing in the early morning hours. The unbearable yowling tears me out of my slumber. I need absolute silence until at least noontime."

She turned toward him and poked her finger at him. "My students, Your Inglorious Grace, will conduct their singing practice according to their proper timetable, regardless of whether you find it convenient, and certainly not whether it fits into your sleeping schedule."

"But I need my beauty sleep—" he protested.

"Then I suggest you sleep when any other God-fearing person does. Good day."

She marched back to her house, certain that red-hot steam puffed out of her ears.

The audaciousness! The arrogance! The insolence!

Why, oh why, did this infuriating man have to live here? What was his aim? What did one have to do to get him to return to London?

An idea occurred to her.

"Martha!"

"Yes, ma'am." The faithful maid appeared immediately.

"Remember the other day Mrs Smythe offered us a rooster and three chickens, and we declined, saying we have no time to care for them?"

"Yes, ma'am. And a shame it is, too, for we could have our very own fresh eggs for breakfast."

"Indeed, so we could. I have changed my mind. Please let Mrs Smythe know we will happily take the chickens. And Martha, put them on the right side of the garden, close to the fence."

"Yes ma'am."

Fresh eggs for breakfast. That was something to look forward to, indeed.

A little smile flitted over her normally austere face.

Then she remembered the duke's smirk.

Those eyes! No doubt this was how he seduced women. He bent forward and stared into his hapless victim's eyes. No wonder the women dropped at his feet like dead flies. Well, not her. Certainly never her.

CHAPTER EIGHT

NOTICE IS HEREBY GIVEN
that all persons are cautioned against unlawfully setting foot on
my property in Paradise Row and Chestnut Street. Any person
caught trespassing will be prosecuted.
Fariq, Esq. p.p. Rochford

Sometimes Marcus wondered whether it was all worth it. The entire house was a construction site. The persistent hammering on the roof felt like an obsessed woodpecker hacking against his skull, and when he fled below-stairs he ran into plasterers and carpenters, stepped onto nails, slipped on freshly waxed boards, and stumbled over pots of paint.

To top it all, he'd had daily visits from the parish. The pastor had been here, together with his wife, inquiring at first with polite solicitousness, whether His Grace had settled down and whether they could be of help; then with increased suspiciousness what plans His Grace had pertaining to the house.

"We are refurbishing it," Fariq shouted in between two volleys of hammering.

"So, I hear," the pastor shouted back, knitting his forehead in worry. "However, it has come to my ears that His Grace intends to open a locality of, um, er, ah, dubious purposes."

Fariq mustered all the diplomacy he was capable of. "'Tis but a misunderstanding. His Grace is here to recuperate and reform his ways."

"Reform his ways, indeed?" The pastor's face brightened.

"Pray, how does he intend to reform his ways?" His wife leaned forward, eager to soak up the newest piece of gossip. The Wicked Duke reforming his ways, imagine!

"Breaking his various addictions is quite a difficult undertaking. He needs much rest and restoration, as the breaking of pernicious habits takes much time and requires much solitude. As I am sure you agree?"

The pastor and his wife agreed. "Very commendable. Very commendable, indeed!"

Fariq held the door open to show them out. "So you will understand that His Grace is unable to greet you, nor will he be amenable to show his face at any kind of social event in the future. Reforming takes much solitude and effort, you see."

The pastor saw and understood.

Fariq closed the door behind them with obvious relief.

Some of the other neighbours had been more difficult to fob off, especially Mrs Benningfield, who seemed to be an opinionated woman and patron of the school, and sincerely concerned about the welfare of the children. "I have heard all about that duke," she said in a shrill voice that rose over the general din of the house. "And while we welcome people of calm, honest, straightforward demeanour as residents of this area, we would be very distressed, indeed, to find that this is not the case."

"Rest assured, madam, that the resident of this house is calm, honest and straightforward." To prove his point, Fariq had bribed her with a selection of Indian honey cardamom cakes, which she'd taken at first suspiciously, then with increasing curiosity.

"This is divine," she gasped.

"It is," Fariq had responded. "Take more." He pushed the plate into her face.

"I must have the recipe," the woman said in between two bites. Fariq was only happy to comply if it meant that they'd won another ally in the neighbourhood.

But That Other Woman simply wouldn't give up. The very next day, she'd set the entire society of Social Reform and Spiritual Improvement on them, which was more difficult to get rid of. Fariq had to buy them off with a hefty donation in exchange for a promise that they would not return.

Then, she pulled out her most powerful weapon: the children. One after the other, they came up to his house, timidly, knocking on the door, and asking politely in little voices whether they might have permission to visit the wishing well.

The answer, of course, was no.

The downcast faces and the shuffling feet with which they dragged themselves back were enough to try anyone's utmost patience.

Marcus supposed the best thing was to return to London. There was no peace to be found here. His mansion in London was big, cool and gloomy, without any noisy workers, zealous pastors, demanding children and griping women.

Even the kitchen was now dominated by women. What was worse, the cook was English. He'd insisted on an Indian cook, but Fariq had wrung his hands and claimed that there was no Indian cook in the entire kingdom available for hire. Marcus preferred his food spicy, so spicy that the mouth burned, or cloyingly sweet. He could live off Turkish delight and chai tea for days on end. Now that he had to forego alcohol altogether, he'd turned to imbibe gallons of tea with milk. But this pap? He lifted the spoon and let the formless thing that appeared to be overcooked cabbage splash back into the bowl, this was a crime to his palate. Maybe if he added some chilli, it would be moderately bearable to eat. After a spoonful of the revolting pap, he'd pushed the bowl away. The footman, who'd brought him the bowl, was nowhere in sight. Was there nothing here to wash the taste away? The decanter with the brandy was empty, and he'd finished his tea. He made his way down to the kitchen.

The stout woman, he surmised, seemed to be the cook, for she was standing in front of a blubbering cauldron, stirring something that smelled loathsomely like cabbage stew. The other two were kitchen maids. A sallow-looking girl kneaded bread, and the other girl, thin as a twig, peeled potatoes.

"Your Grace!" the cook put her hands on her hips. "You must summon the footman. I can't have you come down here every time you need something."

He grumbled. Another snippy, griping, scolding woman. He had enough of that kind. Specifically, that one next door, the one with the flashing eyes and the claws. Madame Puss. "I just want a glass of cold milk. If I may."

The cook pressed a glass of milk into his hands and shooed him out of the kitchen.

He went upstairs and nearly stumbled over the painter, who crouched on the floor with a pot of paint, painstakingly painting the skirting boards.

"Careful! Watch it, guv'nor."

He took a left and went into the drawing room, seeing to his relief that the hole in the floor had been repaired and the monstrous dresser was back in its old place.

He shut the door and threw himself into an armchair.

Ah. What he wouldn't give for a good glass of whiskey.

Instead, he had this.

Milk.

He sipped from the glass and sighed.

Far he'd fallen, indeed. His cronies in the clubs would slap their hands on their thighs and roll on the floor, laughing, if they saw him now.

It couldn't be helped. He'd sworn to change this infernal addiction, and he did.

Well, almost. The craving returned, now and then, but he could handle it so much better than before.

He stared moodily into the glass.

All because of a dream.

He groped his hand in his breast pocket and pulled out a trinket. It was a silver oval locket pendant intricately engraved with a chain attached to it. Closed, it looked like a pretty piece of feminine jewellery to be worn around the neck. Marcus pressed a little hidden button to reveal the tiny picture tucked inside.

He stared at it in despair. The dark-haired Indian

princess with an enigmatic smile looked nothing like the real person.

The familiar old pain rushed through him.

There were no words for Adika's beauty. She had been ethereal, glorious, a goddess. She'd possessed a gentle, kind personality, with wise eyes that saw the best in everyone, including himself.

He'd fallen desperately, painfully, in love with her.

Yet she'd been married.

To his best friend, John.

John had been one of those naive men who believed in the good of all mankind. He'd had such an innocent, optimistic outlook on life that Marcus wondered how a man like him ever managed to survive in this brutal world. He'd always felt protective of John.

John had gone to India, and Marcus never thought his friend could survive a single day there. But John surprised everyone. He'd developed a passion for the country and its people.

"You have to come here, Marcus. It is incredible. This is an entirely different world, and I am sure you would love it. Do come," he wrote.

After his fiasco in London—he'd shot the husband of the woman he'd seduced earlier—though one could argue it had been the other way around—it had been an honest mistake—the seduction, not the shooting, for she'd told him she was a widow. No matter, a lot of water had gone under the bridge in the meantime, yet he still cringed at the memory of the look on his father's face, who'd deemed it necessary for him to disappear for a while. So, he'd decided it was a prime idea to join John in India.

John, who had married and integrated so much into

the local life and culture, he'd fairly become an Indian himself. It had been splashed all over the news, as the most romantic, incredible and outrageous story of the year: Captain John Reid had married a real Indian princess and turned Indian himself.

Oh, the scandal!

Marcus had wanted to see that with his own eyes.

So, he joined John in Bombay.

They'd met him at the port, John and his wife, Adika.

One look at her and he'd fallen hard. He'd thought he'd known love before, but it was nothing, nothing compared to this!

This agony, this longing.

The hopelessness of it all.

Yet he'd loved John, too, by George.

It had torn him apart, for by loving his wife, he was unfaithful to his friend.

But despite the scoundrel that he was, he'd never, ever, betrayed his friend. No matter how hard his heart clamoured, begged, desired, or howled.

He, who had neither principles nor scruples in life, had sworn that this is where he would draw his line. That was the only principle he'd ever adhered to. And it had led him to his doom.

He rubbed his forehead wearily between his finger and thumb. How long ago it was.

Adika and John were long dead. They had died in a terrible earthquake, and only their daughter and he had survived it. And as much as he'd wanted to, he'd never dreamed about either of them.

Until recently.

He'd engaged in his usual activity and caroused

through the night, at a particularly wild orgy held by one of his cronies. It had been bad before, but this time, it had been beyond everything. He'd passed out under the table and remained there for an entire day.

The dream had lasted minutes, maybe even seconds. It had been more a flash of a vision. He dreamed he'd awoken with a massive headache. He'd taken in the destruction in the room, the stench of the sweat and vomit emitted by the bodies sprawled about on the floor, unconscious in an alcoholic stupor. His glance had wandered to the window—there she stood. As clear and real and alive as she'd ever been. The golden morning light flowed about her, and he saw every detail of her dress, every fold, the curl of her hair around her ears, the golden bracelets on her arms, the red dot between her brows.

"Adika," he croaked.

She turned her head, and the look on her face punched his gut.

"Oh, Marcus. What has become of you?" Even as she whispered, she became translucent as the light shone through her, brighter and brighter, until she disappeared and there remained but the window and the morning sun shining through it.

The entire experience left him shaken to his very core.

That look on her face nearly killed him. Such sadness, such regret. He shuddered. Was that what Adika would think of him if she were still alive?

What has become of you? The words had burned themselves into his brain.

What had become of him, indeed? His life was one gigantic pile of manure, and sometimes he surprised himself he hadn't shot a bullet through his brains yet, though he had considered it, once or twice.

When he was a child, his father had told him to seize the day and see as much of the world as possible. He'd been as naive as John, but full of passion and excitement for what the world had to offer.

What had become of that bright, eager boy?

He covered his face in his hands.

A series of small missteps and misguided decisions. A life lived too fast, too wild.

But why?

To outrun death.

There'd been so many. Too many violent deaths.

His mother, who'd died in childbirth. His brother, who'd fallen through the ice in front of him when he was ten. Adika. John. The earthquake. His father, who they say, found his early grave grieving a son who'd lost his way.

Everyone he ever loved had all died before their time.

It was as if he were cursed.

What has become of you?

They all thought he was the wicked duke because he was a dissolute, hard-hearted scoundrel and incapable of loving. Yet the opposite was true.

His love was too deep, too profound, too intense. It killed people, and that was enough to drive anyone insane.

That morning, he'd walked through half of London, shattered and shaken to his very core, realising that he had to make a decision. He could let his curse drive him insane. Give himself the bullet. Or defy it all and attempt to change things before it was too late.

He knew Adika would've wanted him to choose the latter.

He would have to change his ways.

And that was really why he was here, in Bath. He gulped down the last remains of his milk, grimaced, and set the glass aside. Cut himself loose from the past and his old self.

He doubted it was possible.

But he had to try.

A knock on the door jerked him out of his reverie.

"Ah, here you are." Fariq entered, impeccably polished as ever in a Weston coat and Hoby boots. He'd left off his turban this time, and his black hair was slicked back with oil.

Marcus tilted his head to the side and regarded him thoughtfully. "Fariq."

"The workers are almost done for the day, and we can proceed to acquire more furniture. Although it should have arrived long ago. It is vexatious. I have ordered billiard and faro tables. The deuce knows what happened to them because they have vanished."

"Have you ever regretted that I picked you up on that street in Bombay?"

Fariq blinked. "Every single day. Where would I be without you? Roaming the streets, unshackled, free, and without a care in the world, instead of devoting every minute of my free time to a cantankerous old duke."

"You'd also be poor, starving, and possibly dead."

Fariq lifted a finger. "Possibly, you are right. Or I might be happily married to a fine woman with ten children."

"And living in abject poverty. Instead, you are the

former valet of the notorious Duke of Rochford and one of the richest men in all of London, if not England, and the owner of the illustrious Perpignol."

"Thanks to your gambling skills, which you have taught me." Fariq pulled out a pack of cards and flipped them through his fingers. "Want to play?"

"No."

"Don't tell me you'll give up gambling as well as alcohol, opium, and womanising?"

"No one said anything about giving up womanising, and as for gambling, I am in the middle of setting up a gaming hell, am I not? Remind me why I am doing this? I must have maggots in my brain." He pressed two fingers between his brows.

"I think so, too." Fariq sat down next to him and kept shuffling his cards. "I have been thinking about it. It's The Woman. You like her."

There was no doubt about who he meant.

"I do not!"

Fariq lifted a hand. "Yes, you do. You are just doing this to tease her. That means you like her." He laughed at the outrage on Marcus's face.

"She is a cold, starchy, prim, prissy schoolmistress. Sharp-tongued, sharp-clawed and sharp-eyed, full of cutting edges where there should be curves. She is entirely unpleasant to deal with. And you're telling me I like her? I like my women soft, curvy, and biddable."

"And stupid."

Marcus glowered at him.

"But this one is anything but stupid." Fariq flipped the card between his fingers. It was a queen of hearts. "She has a sharp brain, too. She's a worthy match. If she were a gamester, I would like to play against her. And she's got you in her shackles."

Marcus shot out of his chair. "Now there you are entirely wrong."

"Admit it. You were about to leave town when she came along. Suddenly you were eager to reform the house and turn this hovel into a gaming salon, just to vex her."

"Even if that were so, why are you playing along? You have more important business to tend to in London."

Fariq was quiet for a moment. "I think you need the distraction. I didn't like where you were going before."

"And where have I been going?" Marcus invested a heavy dose of sarcasm in his voice, but he was curious about Fariq's response.

Fariq set down his cards. "It's certainly not been a walk through the park. I don't know what happened, Marcus, to make you decide to change your ways from one day to the next. I only know that it was about time. The proverbial five minutes before midnight. You were about to jump into the jaws of hell, and somehow, you decided to step away from the precipice. There must have been a reason, but I won't ask you to divulge it."

Marcus looked grimly out of the window but did not say anything.

"You saved me from poverty and certain death in Bombay," Fariq continued. "You're my only family. A father and a brother. But most of all, my best friend. So, if there is anything at all that I can do to keep you away from that precipice, I will do it." He placed a hand over his heart and bowed. "With everything I have."

Marcus cleared his throat once, twice. Blinked his

eyes. Cleared his throat again. "Hm." That was all he got out.

Fariq clapped him on his shoulder. "Do you need another glass of milk, Your Grace? A footstool? More light? A blanket?"

"What am I, an invalid or an old man?"

Fariq tilted his head sideways. "Both?"

"Go to hell, Fariq."

Fariq laughed. Then he bent forward, narrowed his eyes and spied out of the window. "What in blazes?"

"What?"

"Something is moving about in the garden. And it's not the workers, because these people are wearing dresses."

Marcus looked outside. Indeed, between the birch trees on the right, he saw flashes of blue scurry by. "Blast it, it's an invasion! Now they are sneaking to the wishing well in plain daylight. I thought you closed the hole in the fence."

"I did, but they must have either reopened it or found another way to get through. Those brats are like little insects, they multiply mysteriously. Squash ten of them one day, and a hundred return the next. Then they go about scurrying through every nook and cranny, little weasels. Breaks your heart to see their eyes fill with tears when you tell them they're not allowed to visit that well."

"We must protect our land. Go out and catch them, but mind you, don't bash them over the head with the poker. I want them alive. Trap them and lock them into the dungeon. We can use them as ransom."

Fariq uttered a laugh. "Ye dukes and your infernal need to protect the land. How mediaeval! Dungeon, indeed! The broom closet is more like it."

Marcus attempted to slap the side of his head, but he evaded him. "Go catch them."

Fariq gave a military salute and stormed out of the room.

Marcus watched through the window as Fariq tried to go after them, but the girls, for girls no doubt they must be, dispersed in all directions, shrieking. They probably thought it was a great sport, too. Look at him! He seemed to enjoy himself as well. It was a big game of chase. When three of those brats threw themselves at him, Fariq tumbled to the ground, and the rest threw themselves on top, screeching and giggling delightedly.

Marcus snorted. He would have to close that hole in the fence himself to prevent further incursions onto his property. And set up armed guards. A sign, "Any intruders will be prosecuted, thrown into prison and tortured," might also be a good idea. He would have to tell Fariq to do all three.

CHAPTER NINE

WANTED

Exclusive Gambling Establishment seeking single females for an exceptionally well-paid position. Paradise Row 26 and Chestnut Street.

*T*he next morning, the most awful sound imaginable tore him out of his slumber.

A shriek in a pitch he'd hitherto thought impossible rent through the air, causing him to tear from his bed with his heart nearly jumping out of his chest. The note wavered in the air, demanding and plaintive. It sounded like a slaughtered pig that refused to die, for the note kept wavering on and on.

"By Jove! What is that infernal noise? Are we under attack? Fariq!" He reached for his pistol, which wasn't where it was supposed to be.

Once more, the scream rent through the air. He gritted his teeth and clamped his hands over his ears.

Fariq stormed into the room. He was wearing his nightshirt, and his long locks tumbled about his shoulders. "What? What?"

"Listen." Marcus lifted a finger.

Fariq listened.

A third shriek cut through the air.

Even Fariq, with nerves of steel, cringed. "By Kali's beard. I've heard a lot of things in my life, but this tops it all. On the other hand, we are in the country, after all."

"The last time I checked, I thought we were in a reasonably civilised town called Bath."

"If you please, sir. I grew up in Bombay. Bath is a farmer's village compared to Bombay."

Marcus opened the window. "Stop this infernal noise!" he bellowed, to no avail.

"This animal was definitely not here before." Fariq looked at him with wide eyes. "Do you think The Woman obtained it just to pester you?"

"Of course she did." Marcus breathed heavily.

Another shriek.

"That woman is driving me to insanity!" he roared. "Fariq! My pistol!"

"Are you going to shoot her now?"

"Yes. After I've shot that blasted chicken."

"A male chicken who crows is commonly called a rooster."

"Fariq!"

"Your Grace?"

"Don't you dare."

"Dare what?" Fariq looked at him with wide eyes.

"Become schoolmistress-ish on me. She may be a haberdasher of pronouns, but you are not."

"I can't help it. It does seem to rub off on one somehow—all right, all right." Fariq lifted both hands with a grin. "Your pistol is in the bottom drawer."

Marcus fetched his pistol and marched outside with a murderous face.

He headed straight to the fence near the wishing well. Looking over the boxwood hedge, he could indeed see that there was a chicken coop installed there. Neither the coop nor the chickens had been there yesterday. The rooster sat on top of the hut and glared at him malevolently. It opened its beak for another hideous crow.

Marcus levelled the pistol at the creature. His finger tensed around the trigger.

Then he heard a gasp.

A little girl in a blue gingham gown and an apron stood in front of him, clasping a basket. Jupiter only knew where she'd suddenly come from. She must've grown from the ground like a toadstool. She had black curls and was no older than five or six years old. Her mouth was agape, her eyes two porcelain-blue discs full of reproach.

He couldn't shoot the animal with that girl watching. He lowered the pistol.

"You're not going to thoot Jameth?" She lisped in a high little voice.

"Jameth? You named the blasted rooster James?" That struck him as so ridiculous that he forgot his anger.

The girl looked at him severely. "You thould not thay bad wordth." She pointed at the animals in order. "Jameth, Matilda, Jethica, and Evangelithta."

"You gave his harem names, too?"

"Oh yeth. And I am to pick up eggth for breakfatht. But if you are going to thoot Jameth, that'th not very nice."

Her lower lip wobbled.

Marcus scratched his head. If there was one thing he could not stand, it was a child's tears, especially if they hung on long eyelashes like dewdrops on grass blades. It made him uncomfortable and edgy, and he liked neither feeling. Aware that he still held his pistol, he handed it to Fariq, who'd come running after him.

Then the sounds of off-key singing and a badly tuned piano carried loudly through an open window.

Both Marcus and Fariq winced.

"Didn't I tell that infernal woman to move her music classes to another time of the day?"

The rooster started up again as if wanting to join in the chorus.

"This is unbearable." Marcus cringed as the chorus sang a particularly loud, discordant melody. "Do you know what time it is?"

The girl looked at him with wide eyes. "They are prac-tithing hymnth before breakfatht."

"Hymns! Before breakfast! You must be joking."

"It ith our new routine," the girl explained.

"Hah! I knew it! She is doing this on purpose!"

"I am not!" The little girl placed her hands on her hips and glowered at him.

"I don't mean you. I mean *her*." Marcus gnashed his teeth so hard it was a miracle he did not grind them to powder.

As if remembering why she was there, the little girl

opened the gate of the coop and went inside. "I have to get the eggth!"

"It is the middle of the night, and one ought to let a person sleep, not collect eggth, I mean, eggs," he retorted.

"Why are you tho croth?" She tilted her head sideways as she studied him.

"Croth?"

"I think she means cross," Fariq translated as he leaned against the fence.

"I'm not cross." Marcus shot an irritated look at the school. "I just want to sleep. I get cranky when I don't get enough sleep."

The girl nodded sympathetically. "Me too." She placed the eggs carefully into the basket and smiled at him. "You know what? You are croth, but I like you anyhow." With those words, she scurried back to the house whence she'd come.

"Forevermore, the womaniser," Fariq commented. "Another conquest."

"Bah." Marcus stalked back to the house when the rooster and chorus started up again with a hostile medley.

"This is it. There will be consequences." He turned on his heel, changed his direction, and marched through the front garden.

"What are you going to do?" Fariq called after him.

"Shoot the headmistress," Marcus opened the iron gate with such force it banged against the fence.

"Good that I have the pistol, then." Fariq strolled back to their house, whistling a tune from the off-note hymn.

Marcus hammered on the door of the seminary. A peaky-looking maid opened and froze as her eyes travelled down his body and jerked up again to his face.

"I want to talk to Miss Princum Prancum."

"Who?" There were speckled flecks of crimson on her cheeks.

"That schoolmistress of yours." He waved an impatient hand.

"We have three. There is Miss Robinson, Miss Everglade and Miss Johnson."

"There's a fourth one. Miss Hilverbrandt."

"You mean, our headmistress, Miss Hilversham?"

"Whoever."

"If you would wait in the drawing room, sir," the maid finally moved aside and led him to a simple yet elegant green drawing room. Green velvet curtains draped the windows, and a sofa, chairs and a walnut coffee table stood in the middle of the room. A painting of what looked like a Turner hung over the fireplace.

Hah! What did his eyes behold? There was a faro table standing by the window. It was so new that the acrid wood polish stung his nose. Here was the missing furniture Fariq had been complaining about earlier. She'd stolen it.

"To whom do I owe this dubious honour?"

He pivoted on his heel to face The Woman, who paused by the door, looking cool and collected as ever.

"Ah. It is you." Her eyes went coolly up and down his figure, and her fine nose wrinkled. "Martha?"

"Yes, ma'am." The maid toyed with the strings of her apron and doggedly refused to look at him.

"Fetch His Grace a shirt and a coat. I believe we have one hanging in Mr Tiverton's former room."

He looked down at himself, realising for the first time what a figure he must make. Dash it if he hadn't forgotten to dress. He was wearing his banyan, which hung open, revealing his bare chest. At least he'd remembered to pull on a pair of trousers. That was, no doubt, the reason the maid had ogled him in that manner.

He couldn't say he had the same reaction on The Woman. She seemed more put off than attracted to him. He had no idea why that thought irked him.

She folded her hands, and her eyes behind her spectacles glittered.

"You stole my furniture," Marcus pointed a finger at the faro table.

"We did not." Of course, she had to use pronouns like the queen.

"Don't tell me you play faro with your students."

"And why not? We use it to teach the probability of gambling and the unlikelihood of winning."

He snorted. "They've misdelivered the furniture, or rather, you have convinced them to deliver it here, so you hampered us in setting up our gambling club."

"What devious motives you consign us to have! Do you have any proof?"

Marcus had to accede that he did not. "No."

She folded her hands in front of her. "Since I gather you did not come here to make false claims, then to what do I owe this visit?"

"Make that ear-deafening racket stop."

"I beg your pardon?"

The rooster crowed again.

"That."

"Oh. You mean James. He is our newest resident here, together with—"

"Belinda, Helen and Perdita. Or was it Evangelista? I

have been informed all about them by one of your illustrious students."

She raised a fine eyebrow. "Oh, have you?" Her brow cleared. "You mean Little May. She is our youngest one. She was fetching the eggs this morning."

"Mark my words, ma'am." He jabbed a finger in her direction. "I know precisely what you are doing. You got this creature to irritate me and drive me away. But it won't work. If you don't get rid of this tone-deaf chicken immediately, I will have coq-au-vin for supper tonight."

She looked down her narrow nose from illustrious heights and sniffed. "Might I remind you that a chicken that crows is commonly called—"

"Don't you dare say it!"

"—a rooster." She looked smug.

The chorus started up again. He winced. "As for this, I told you to move the chorus hours to another time of the day."

"I tell you what, Your Grace. Let me give you a tour of the house, so you can see with your own eyes what my students are up to."

"I don't want a blasted tour of the house."

"But of course you do." The calculating look in her eyes made him pause.

"Do I?"

"Why, yes. You have never actually seen the school, have you? Yet you have paid a fortune for it."

"Did I?"

"Penelope's tuition lasted for seven years. Which was not little, if I may say so."

He did not know how much he had paid for his former

ward's tuition. He'd never bothered to ask his secretary about it.

"You must be curious about what you have invested in. So let me show you." Miss Hilversham's voice dripped with saccharine.

He was about to tell her he didn't give a fig for how she had invested the money that she had extorted from him, when the maid entered, bearing items of clothing.

"But first, you need to dress yourself."

The maid handed him the coat and a shirt. He took both, grumbling.

"Ma'am, there's a situation in Miss Everglade's classroom. If you could come. It is rather urgent." A girl in a blue gingham dress, no doubt an older student, had entered the room. She looked at him with wide eyes.

"If you will excuse me, I need to see to this matter. I will return shortly." Miss Hilversham took the girl by the arm and left with quick, firm steps. He remained behind in the drawing room with his faro table, wearing someone else's coat.

The shrieking continued outside and inside the walls.

Then a hammering started up from the rooftops.

What was this place? A madhouse?

It was a madhouse.

It pained her to admit that the duke was right. The new music teacher had no experience in teaching, and judging from the barbarous sounds emerging from the music room, he could not tell the difference between *allegro* and *andante* either. James, the rooster, had no sense of timing whatsoever, for he crowed from dawn till dusk.

Nonstop. His crow was not a proper, punctual crow as roosters are wont to produce, but an atrocious sound that bore no description. This, no doubt, was the reason Mrs Smythe had wanted to get rid of him and the other chickens. Fresh eggs for breakfast were an advantage, of course, but that was about it. Then, the leakage on the roof was being repaired. Finally, some workers had arrived to see to the hole in it. Hence, the intermittent hammering.

To top it all, one of Miss Everglade's students was having a fit. Rosa had the falling sickness. She had a tendency to fall and shake and foam at the mouth. If only the remaining students would remain reasonable while the fit lasted, but no. They invariably broke out in horrified shrieks and sobbed along, as if that would help the poor child recover. And Miss Everglade, instead of remaining calm and collected as a teacher ought in such a situation, broke down, sobbing along in sympathy.

It was enough to drive anyone insane.

Eleonore gritted her teeth.

Of all times, that overbearing duke had to appear half-naked with his chiseled Grecian chest and murderously handsome face and immediately recognised his faro table. Maybe it had not been such a good idea to offer him a tour of the school as he would see the billiard table in the library as well.

Eleonore had to be honest with herself and admit that he was entirely in the right. The racket was unbearable, and those tables were, after all, his.

When all the chaos and crying died down, she hoped he could be brought to reason, even though she doubted that something like reason was to be found behind that sardonic smile of his.

She stepped into Miss Everglade's classroom and found her bent over a girl who was lying on the floor.

"Stop the crying this instant," Eleonore commanded as she took charge of the situation. "Mary, tell Mr Nonni to pause his music lessons and to come here. I need his help. Mary, open the window; Rosa needs some air."

After the children had calmed down, Rosa snapped out of her fit and looked around disoriented, before falling back into a deep sleep on the sofa. There was order and silence once more on the school premises (if only James were to learn his timetable better!), so Eleonore returned to the duke.

Where on earth was he? Had he left?

"I don't think so, ma'am," Martha replied. "He asked for a glass of milk."

"Milk?"

"Yes ma'am."

Puzzled, she went to the library, only to find it empty. He wasn't in any of the other two drawing rooms, either. From one classroom, she heard a deep, male voice.

Her steps increased.

He was in Mr George's geography class.

Sitting easily on the table, with one leg dangling down, he gestured with one hand as he spoke, while the entire class, including Mr George, listened in rapt silence.

"Now, Humayun was not only a great ruler and brilliant military strategist, he was also responsible for some of the greatest Mughal architectural masterpieces. Humayun's tomb is one of a kind. His wife had it built. Let me tell you the tale that goes with it...."

Eleonore listened, half in awe, to his gripping tale of how Humayun's grieving wife had dedicated her remaining life to having his mausoleum built.

He then picked up a piece of chalk and sketched the layout of the tomb in octagonal shapes.

One hand shot into the air.

"You. What is your name?"

"Priscilla, sir."

"Very well, Priscilla. What is it you want to know?"

"I was wondering, sir, whether what you say can be true, that there can be a love so strong, so all-powerful that it could survive beyond death and into all eternity."

His face underwent a subtle transformation. It hardened, yet his eyes suddenly looked bleak. He stared out of the window.

Silence settled over the classroom.

"Sir?"

He snapped his head toward her as if he'd forgotten where he was. "Of course, it is all nonsense." He threw the chalk on the desk so that it broke in half. "Forget everything I told you. The ultimate lesson today is that you should never give your heart away, because you'll end up building a tomb where it'll rot for all eternity." He spied Eleonore standing by the door. He got up, bowed, and walked over to her. "End of lesson."

"But sir! But sir!" a chorus of voices started up in protest.

He ignored them and followed her out into the hallway.

"That was quite interesting." Eleonore assessed him.

He brushed it away. "I gathered some knowledge on my trip through India. When I passed by the classroom, and I heard that moron declare that the Mughal empire was founded by Shah Jahan, I had to intervene. The man has no idea what he is talking about. I must say, I am rather disappointed at the quality of your teachers, Miss Hilvermam."

"Hilversham." She glared at him.

He stopped in front of the mural by the stairs.

"Now this is prime art. Greek mythology, yes?"

"This mural was started by the artist P.J Tiverton and completed by my students. As you can see, not everything in my school is of inferior quality."

"I have heard of the fellow. It seems to be in fashion in London these days to have a Tiverton hanging over the fireplace. He taught here?"

"For a while. He is married to one of my teachers now."

She ushered him into a drawing room. The truth was that her best teachers either left or were married, and she had great difficulty in replacing them.

"Well, Miss Hilverjam. What are we to do now?"

She smiled at him sweetly. "I suggest you consider my offer once more regarding the property swap, and your problems will, with one fell swoop, be eliminated."

"You never give up, do you?" A gleam of amusement stole into his green eyes.

"I do not."

"Then we are at an impasse, madam." He took off Mr Tiverton's coat and handed it to her. He kept on the shirt and picked up his red morning coat and shrugged into it. "For I intend to go ahead with my plans. I have invested far too much into the renovation of the house."

At this, she lost all patience.

"I don't understand why you won't see reason. What benefit do you have from doing this?"

He shrugged. "Money? Women? Both?"

She drew her lips into a derisive line. "Of course. No doubt you have endless experience with both."

"That is understood." He inspected his fingernails. "But that is a topic a woman like you is not likely to understand."

"A woman like me?"

He blithely ignored the warning in her voice. "Of the priggish sort."

The taut, tenuous strings inside her snapped. "How dare you insult me in this manner? I warn you, Your Grace, I won't have it."

"You warn me? What is supposed to happen?"

"I will have the entire neighbourhood coming after you."

"Has already happened. What else?"

"I will inform the Society of Reform that there is a worthy cause right here that needs to be seen to."

"They dropped by yesterday and left with a nifty donation. They promised to leave us in peace. Admit it, there is nothing you can do but accept the fact that we can't have everything we want in life, and that's the way it is. Now, before you have a fit of the vapours, may I suggest you tell your servants to deliver my furniture to my house, where it belongs."

Eleonore nearly lost her temper.

He looked at her pensively. "Did you know you look rather beautiful when you are angry? Madame Puss. Beneath that prim and proper façade is a hellcat."

"Don't call me that!"

He stepped up to her, and suddenly there was a challenging gleam in his eyes.

"Madame Hellcat," he said in a husky voice. "I like it." Then he lowered his face and kissed her on her lips.

It came so fast and unexpected, and it was such a surprisingly soft and sweet kiss, that Eleonore was momentarily taken aback.

He looked up and blinked. "Let me try this again." He gathered her in his arms and kissed her once more.

For one half a second, she was tempted to respond. For half a second, she allowed herself to melt in his arms and savour the delicious sensation of being thoroughly kissed.

Then she struggled away, raised her hand, and smacked it across his cheek with a resounding slap.

He didn't seem to feel the slap at all, as he kept staring at her as if thunderstruck.

He rubbed his neck. "I think this was a mistake."

"How dare you?" Her voice shook.

"Educational, but definitely a mistake," he muttered.

"Of course, from a licentious man like you, I shouldn't have expected any different behaviour. Going about k-k-k-kissing women like that."

He looked at her as if he saw her for the first time. "Of course, I go about and just randomly kiss women. Any kind of woman, as long as she wears skirts. Opera dancers, serving maids, the fish vendor on the market. Even the prim schoolmistress next door. It's what I do." The cynical gleam was back in his eyes. "So, you need not take this personally at all."

Eleonore felt a flush rise up her neck. First, he had kissed her, and she had to admit, to her chagrin, that it hadn't been such a terrible kiss at all, actually—then he told her not to take it personally? She folded her arms across her chest and struggled to regain some dignity.

"Your Grace, I must ask you to restrain yourself. This is a proper seminary for young ladies. I can't have you coming here half-dressed and k-k-kissing women." Why did she always have to stumble over the word?

"If you weren't so prim and proper, you would see that it is the most natural thing in the world."

"Would you stop calling me that!"

"What would you have me call you instead? Wench? Baggage? Oh, I have it." He lifted a finger. "A Mother of the Maids."

Her eyes threw daggers at him, yet she blushed crimson. "I know what you are implying. I would not have expected anything less of you."

He looked at her innocently. "But that is what you are. A mother of the maids."

She stared into his eyes. "I know very well what that term means. It is an insult of the grossest sort."

"Oh? What does it mean then, I wonder?"

"You imply that I am running a brothel."

"No. Really?" His eyes opened wide in feigned astonishment. "Shocking that you know such indecent slang. Not at all the thing for a prim and proper headmistress to know."

She clenched her hand into a fist to prevent herself from slapping him again.

"You have insulted me in every conceivable way possible. Just in the manner of an immature, foolish, puerile schoolboy," she snapped.

"I am impressed by your vast repertoire of synonyms."

Then he regarded her thoughtfully. "You know what I think? I think you need a man. That would solve all your problems. Yes, I daresay that is what it is. Au revoir, Madame Puss. Miss Hellcat. Until next time."

And with those words, and a dashing smile flashed in her direction, he left, leaving her sputtering for words.

CHAPTER TEN

MATRIMONY

Husband wanted for lonely, uptight headmistress of a girl's school, about 55 years old - shrewd tongue, genteel manners and overly accomplished - anxiously seeking a warm hearth to change her condition and would like to have a husband as soon as possible. Healthy, sober, no bad habits. Fortune is not so much of an object. Letters addressed to Paradise Row 24.

*E*leonore nearly spat her coffee over the breakfast table when she read the announcement in *The Bath Chronicle and Weekly Gazette*. "Ellen, do I need new spectacles or did I read correctly that it says Paradise Row twenty-four?"

Ellen took the newspaper that Eleonore handed to her and read the announcement. A spasm passed over her face. She lifted her hand to her mouth and coughed. "It says twenty-four, indeed. What is this? A prank? Did one of our students place the advertisement?"

"Unlikely. I believe I know who is responsible for this." An angry red speck appeared on Eleonore's cheeks.

"Whoever did this, it is in extremely bad taste."

"Agreed." Eleonore tapped a finger against the tabletop with a rat-at-at-at. "The intent behind this, of course, is to make me lose my calm. He wants nothing more than for me to storm over there and continue fighting. Because he enjoys goading me, you see. Well, I refuse. I refuse to lose my calm. I refuse to get angry. I refuse to allow him to provoke me." Her voice rose in pitch.

Ellen watched her with wide eyes. "I take it you're meaning the duke. Do you think he has placed this advertisement?"

"He most certainly did. He has the maturity of a schoolboy, you see."

"You have certainly roused a tremendous dislike in him. I wonder why?" Ellen creased her forehead. "I would have advised you to back down, but the other day I observed he is serious about installing this gambling club right next to our school. It is insupportable!"

"Unfortunately, we could no longer keep the faro tables after he saw them, and I instructed them to be delivered to his house. Now there is not much to hold him back. What is it you observed, Ellen?" Eleonore paid little attention to what her neighbours were up to the last few days because she had been busy teaching the students, something which she enjoyed tremendously but did not have too much of an occasion to do so. Being a headmistress meant she was responsible for administrative and managerial work. But she'd dismissed the music teacher and now taught the class herself until she could find a replacement.

"A string of people coming and going."

"That might not be anything unusual. Workers, no doubt."

Ellen shifted around in her chair uncomfortably. "They were women. Of a dubious kind."

"Are you certain?"

"No. But the way they were dressed, I would have wagered they were doxies. He isn't about to set up a brothel, in addition to a gambling hell, is he?"

Eleonore sat down her teacup in the saucer with a hard chink. "He wouldn't," she breathed.

Ellen got up and spied out of the window. "There! Look. Another such person." She shook her head. "They can't be serving maids."

Eleonore joined her by the window and looked out. Indeed, a gaudily dressed woman strode up the path to the neighbouring house. She was dressed in scarlet from the plume on her head down to the tip of her slippers. Her dress revealed white, sharp shoulders and a décolleté that was as wide and bare as a windswept field in the highlands. Even from this distance, she could see that the woman's cheeks and lips were brightly rouged.

Eleonore's clutch on the curtains tightened. Somehow, she'd hoped that the duke wasn't as bad as all the rumours had implied. Disappointment churned round and round in her stomach like curdled milk in a butter barrel. She wondered why it mattered so much to her.

It was that kiss, wasn't it?

The memory smouldered and festered and chafed. She hadn't been kissed too often in her life. She could hardly recall when she had last been kissed by a man. Love, kisses, and men had turned out to be such a let-down in her life. They had left her empty, bitter, and convinced her she was altogether better off without them.

Then he'd kissed her and awakened a sense of yearning, an ache accompanied by a fear that she might have been wrong all along.

Suddenly, she'd been aware of the gawping desolation in her life.

Yes, there were people around her all day for whom she was responsible. But behind all that busy hustling, there was a loneliness that she hadn't been aware of until now.

Was this why she resented the duke so much? Not so much because of the kiss itself, but because he highlighted something in her life that was missing?

Maybe he was right.

Maybe she did need love and kisses after all.

Maybe she did need a man.

It was a sobering, humbling thought.

A second woman dressed in moss green with ostrich feathers on her head and her umbrella traipsed up to the house.

Eleonore tightened her lips. "This is intolerable. It is probably entirely illegal, too. He is defiling the entire neighbourhood. We will have to talk to the magistrate. This isn't to be borne."

Ellen chewed on her lips. "I am not sure the magistrate can—or will— do anything about it. Not if he's a duke who is plump in the pockets."

"We will rally the entire neighbourhood and ask the parson to support us. I will write a letter immediately. In the meantime…" An idea occurred to her. She smiled maliciously. "In the meantime, there is something you can do, Ellen, if you please." She bent forward to tell her of her plan.

"Sahib!" Fariq burst into the duke's room.

"For heaven's sake, can't a person get any sleep in this house? First the workers, then all the applicants for the various jobs, then the cursed rooster, and now you. What is the matter now?" Marcus had tossed and turned the entire night and fallen asleep only to be hunted by feverish dreams of Adika, then to be jolted awake by the infernal crowing of the rooster. And now Fariq had crashed into his room just when he'd finally drifted off again. He threw the pillow at him.

Fariq caught it deftly. "It is nearly noontime."

"It's the middle of the night, Fariq. Now, if you will excuse me, I need to sleep." He turned to the other side.

Fariq pulled the blanket away. "We need to do something about the stuff in our front garden."

"What stuff? You are not making any sense. Pray, note that I am starting to feel intensely hostile towards you. Hand me the blanket. It is chilly."

Fariq dropped it on the floor. "You need to come outside and see for yourself. I'm honestly confounded."

Cursing him, Marcus got out of bed, pulled on his banyan and followed him outside.

Fariq hadn't exaggerated. There, in the middle of his front yard, was a steaming pile of manure. Not a small pile as horses were wont to make, but a hill, at least as high as the fence, emitting a stench that rose higher than the tip of the spire of St Paul's.

"Plague and pestilence. What is this?" Marcus gagged and pressed his hand against his nose.

"As you can clearly smell, a pile of sh—" Fariq interrupted himself and cleared his throat. "More importantly, the question is, what are we to do with it?"

"No, Fariq. That isn't the most important question. The more pressing question is, who the blazes left it here? You didn't order fertiliser, did you?"

Fariq scratched his neck. "Not that I can remember. What in thunder does one need it for?"

"Gardening, I suppose."

Fariq's face brightened. "That must be it. The gardener must need it for the garden."

"Except, as far as I know, we haven't hired a gardener yet, have we? Instead, we have had a long string of unsuitable women apply for the position of 'parlour maid'. You should have worded it better in the announcement."

"Why? I wrote something like "Exclusive Gambling Establishment seeking single females for exceptionally well-paid positions." What's wrong with that?"

"The problem, my boy, is that now we have every doxy and prostitute in all of England ringing our doorbell. You should've worded it differently." Marcus shook his head. "Have you at least found anyone suitable?"

"Not yet. In the end, none of the ladies was keen on the position. Who would've known that hiring a plain parlour maid is so difficult? But back to this pile of stink. What do we do about it?"

The duke's eyes wandered pensively to the seminary. "I wonder...?"

Fariq followed his gaze. "No. You think so?"

The duke's eyes narrowed to two hostile chinks of

green. "Do I detect admiration in your voice? 'Pox on her. Who else if not her?"

"That's a rather dirty trick to play. Literally. On the other hand, the garden does need some fertiliser. Once we have hired the gardener, that is. I will see to it immediately. We will have a pond, yes?"

"Do what you must." Marcus waved his hand. "I suggest you have it spread as closely to the neighbour's fence as possible. They should have to wallow in the smell as well." He stomped back to the house. "If this continues, I am going to have their house burned down."

CHAPTER ELEVEN

HELP NEEDED

To clean up fertiliser illegally deposited in my garden. Paradise
Row 24 will pay the bill.

R.

*E*leonore sat in front of the dresser in her nightgown and stared into the oval mirror.

Her room was a refuge, and the only indication that her lineage was genteel. It was a lady's boudoir as befits a proper country house mansion. It was carefully furnished with light blue, striped wallpaper, an elaborate four-poster bed with lace pillows and patchwork blankets lovingly sewn by her students. Attached to the room, through a wall-papered door, was her dressing room.

Eleonore picked up a brush and methodically brushed her silver-blonde hair in slow, rhythmic motions. It was fine, and long, and hung nearly to her waist. Her abigail, Maggie, normally helped her brush it until it shone, but tonight she'd sent the girl to bed early.

"You have hair like a fairy princess," Emma, her nurse, used to tell her. She'd braid it into two braids and wrap them around her head. Sometimes, she put flowers between her plaits and ran outside, barefoot, to play in the forest that bordered her father's estate, pretending she was the fairy queen. Eleonore's eyes glazed over as a memory surfaced.

She is a wild child, the servants in her father's house whispered behind her back. A creature of the woods! She is a forest sprite, an elfin child, with silver hair and silver eyes.

She fished in the brook, rode the horses bareback, and climbed the trees. Her faithful companion was her brother Ned, who was three years younger and mortally afraid of heights. She wheedled him into climbing up the tree anyhow, with her bare feet, promising him her portion of pudding if he dared to follow her.

He did.

"See, it's not so bad!" she told him.

Ned had clung to the branch with a white face.

"Just don't stare down," she'd told him. "Look up, instead. See how blue the sky is? Isn't it wonderful? I wonder whether I can climb to the treetop and touch the clouds?"

He'd turned his head to look up and wrapped his arms and legs firmly around the branch. "I don't know, Violetta. It's so high. I want to go down!" he wailed.

"Oh, very well. I will go first, and you just follow me."

But he'd refused to let go of the branch.

"Let go, otherwise you'll stay there forever," she'd told him.

But he'd shook his head and refused.

After she had returned to the ground, she piled up leaves underneath the tree and told her brother to let himself fall onto the stack.

Ned howled.

"Let go, Ned. Let go! You'll see it won't be so bad. It's quite soft!"

But Ned refused. In the end, he swore he'd stay in the tree even if he had to be up there the entire night, and she had had to go back to the house to fetch the gardener to help him down.

The burly man grumbled as he climbed the tree and carried the boy down on his back.

"Don't go climbing trees, it's not seemly for a lady." He instructed her. "And you, boy, don't climb up anything if you can't get down on your own again."

Ned had sulked.

She'd flung her wild hair back proudly. "I never let anyone tell me what to do."

In the evening, her father, with whom she hardly ever exchanged a word, for he rarely had anything to tell her, called her to his study and told her in his cold, indifferent voice that it was time for her to change her wild ways. He'd hired a governess, and she was to be turned into a lady, have a season, and get married.

"But I am too young to get married!" she'd cried. She was not yet fifteen.

"It is not too early for you to get betrothed," her father had countered.

"Mama?" She turned to her mother, who sat next to him, her face a calm, lovely mask. Her fingers shook as she embroidered, yet there would be no support from her.

"Your father is right, dear." Only a slight tremor in her voice betrayed her uneasiness in the situation. "A governess will be good for you."

"But to get married?"

"Sooner or later, you will have to get married, dear." Her mother had had no choice in the matter, either.

"The governess, a Miss Netherford, is already on the way here. Your days of running about uncontrolled, foraging the forest, are over. Go to your room and stay there and behave like the young lady everyone expects you to be." Her father picked up his quill to indicate that he was done with the conversation.

She left her father's study, stunned.

Her brother Ned skulked in the hallway outside. "Was it bad?"

She licked her dry lips. "He wants to turn me into a lady and make me marry someone. A stranger."

"That's terrible," Ned said. "But that's what girls are supposed to do, I suppose."

Ned was only a boy. He had a tutor, but outside his tutoring hours, he was allowed to run free. It was expected of him to prove his mettle. Yet he did not have half the courage to do the things that his big sister did.

It wasn't fair.

She narrowed her eyes. "Not me. Never."

He looked at her with alarm. "What are you going to do?"

She lifted her chin in determination. "I will run away."

ELEONORE'S HAND HAD DROPPED LONG AGO AS SHE KEPT staring into the oval mirror, no longer seeing her reflection in it. Why were these memories coming up now? She hadn't thought of Ned, her domineering father, or her loving, but weak mother in a very long time. She'd banished those memories of her childhood like wisps of a dream.

Those memories were from a different world, from a

different life. She was no longer The Honourable Violetta Winford, the beautiful, wild, but headstrong daughter of Baron Leighton, who'd run away to London to her beloved godmother, only to find her ruin there.

She wondered whether things would've been different if she hadn't run away. If she'd stayed and allowed herself to be turned into the biddable girl her parents so wanted. Married off at sixteen.

Violetta had been determined to take fate into her own hands. Violetta, who was drawn to everything that was forbidden, knew no rules and regulations. She'd treasured freedom beyond everything.

She'd paid dearly for it.

She'd toppled into a hole so deep and terrible and ferocious that when she had finally clawed herself out of it, she was no longer the free, wild spirited Violetta Winford.

She had become Eleonore Hilversham.

The capable, efficient, strict, cool, prim headmistress, firmly in charge of not only her own life but everyone else's. Control over her little empire was everything. Control over her emotions, control over her life.

Her hand clamped around the silver hairbrush so tightly that her knuckles whitened.

Eleonore was everything Violetta despised.

Sometimes, she thought, she saw the imp who was Violetta still lurking in the depths of her eyes. Sometimes, she still felt her stir, but she quickly pushed her down.

But lately, she'd come to the surface more than once, tugging at her, clamouring for attention.

Why was that?

It was that duke, that infernal duke.

He'd kissed her, and that kiss had done something to her. He'd rattled on a door that she'd firmly shut and forgotten.

He'd somehow stirred in her soul and dug up her passions, the rebellion, and the joy for life—that was Violetta. He reminded her of desires she'd long forgotten, dreams of forbidden adventures and travels to exotic places. All those things that had been denied to her because she was a woman.

Violetta would have adored him.

Eleonore hated him.

She hated those fascinating emerald-green eyes that regarded her as if she were alternately amusing and puzzling to him. She noted the fine crinkles in the corner of his eyes when he truly smiled, which he'd done only once or twice, yet his lips were pulled in a world-weary, perpetual sneer.

He had the mind of an immature schoolboy, the kind who enjoyed pulling a little girl's braids and sticking out his leg to make them trip, simply to laugh when they fell.

She knew that kind. How well she knew them! They knew how to make women fall in love with them.

Only to turn and leave when they were done with them.

Eleonore shuddered. She'd sworn never to have anything to do with that type ever again.

Violetta, innocent, wild, adventurous Violetta, would have fallen for him at the snap of a finger.

But Eleonore knew better. She saw him for what he was: degenerate, licentious, and altogether wicked.

SHE TOSSED AND TURNED, THOUGHTS CHASED BY WORRIES, fears, and what-ifs.

Her school wasn't doing badly at all, yet she knew she needed to push it to the next level. She needed to find excellent teachers who were as committed to the school as she was. Too many were coming, only to leave again. She'd always thought that Frances Littleworth, one of her dearest teachers, would take over the school one day, and she'd coached her in all matters of management and administration. Then Frances had left to marry an earl, and Eleonore had never been able to fill the hole Frances had left behind. Many teachers had come and gone in the meantime.

Eleonore was thankful that Ellen was still here. Ellen Robinson was a steadfast presence. She was not only a reliable teacher but also a friend.

Pearls of sweat formed on Eleanore's neck and chest. She pushed the blankets away. It was an uncommonly warm night, and she got out of bed to open the window and let in the cool night air. Except even with the window open, the air was stifled and thick, as if a thunderstorm were brewing but not ready to unload itself. Her head ached from the tension in the air.

She stared across the garden and wondered whether the duke was sleeping. Unlikely, for his kind caroused and womanised throughout the entire night. Ellen had counted five doxies walking up to his door that day. Five! That was enough to open a bordello.

Then she scolded herself for thinking of him yet again. He wasn't worthy of her thoughts.

Yet she couldn't tear her eyes away from the neighbouring mansion, which was but a dark shadow beyond the trees. She'd placed so many hopes and dreams on it. Were they all to be blown to smithereens because of the wilfulness of a duke? What did the property mean to him?

Nothing.

What did it mean to her?

Everything.

It was her future. Her school was her world.

She felt fiercely responsible and protective of all the souls that lived under her roof, teachers and children alike. Especially the children. She cared deeply for each of them as if they were her own.

But she'd noticed, lately, that she was feeling unsettled. She'd spent nearly half a year with a former student in Scotland, helping her set up another school. The challenge of it all had invigorated her. After she'd returned from the north, she felt restless.

Was this yet another reason she wanted to acquire the property and expand the school? Because she was getting bored with what she had?

Because … it was no longer enough?

A bolt of fear chilled her to the marrow. Could it be that the world she'd so painstakingly built up was now too small?

What was the alternative then?

What did she want?

A husband and children? The fate she'd run away from as a young girl?

She stood up, walked over to the commode, pulled out the drawer, and removed the mahogany box.

The velvet pouch inside was worn out from handling.

A little lock of silken hair fell out onto her palm.

She placed it against her cheek.

"Sleep well, Hope," she whispered.

It had become her nightly ritual to kiss it.

Still hot and restless, she decided to go to the kitchen for a glass of cold milk. She opened her bedroom door and stepped out into the hallway.

Her hand was on the rail of the staircase when she paused. There was a noise upstairs. Were the maids still awake? What was this odd flicker of light in the hallway?

"Martha?" She leaned forward, looking up, but there was no response.

Determined to find out its source, she took the stairs up to the servants' quarters.

CHAPTER TWELVE

SEEKING

new home for rooster. Contact Miss Hilversham at Paradise
Row.

*M*arcus tossed and turned and dreamt of
India.

Night after night, he experienced it again. The earth-
quake, the shaking, the crumbling of the walls, the fire.
Bodies everywhere, dusty, grey. The broken body of
Adika. Her red sari.

The black, merciless hole afterwards.

Marcus groaned and gasped, writhed and struggled
with the blankets, and threw the pillows on the ground.

It was too hot. He sat up in bed and looked around,
disoriented. His eyes fell on a hideous walnut dresser with
a porcelain bowl and his shaving mirror on top. It took
him a moment to comprehend that he was back in

England; cool, rainy England. In that cursed house, in that cursed town. He sighed.

Light flickered through his bedroom window.

It can't be morning already, can it?

He got up, stumbled over a pillow, and drew aside the curtains.

Tongues of orange flames licked the charcoal blackness of the sky. He stared at it with incomprehension. Was this India all over again? Then his brain registered what he was seeing.

The school was burning.

Tugging at his hair with both hands in disbelief, he questioned his sanity. Had he, with the mere uttering of a thoughtless wish earlier, set the school ablaze?

He tore the bedroom door open and roared: "Fariq! Fire!"

Fariq hurtled out of his room, half-dressed, swinging a poker stick. "What? Where?"

"The blasted school is burning."

He bolted through the garden onto the street, where he heard shrieks and shouts. The people who had gathered pointed up at the school. The roof was fully aflame and appeared about to collapse.

Some teachers and a handful of children tumbled through the door, coughing. Several maids huddled together, weeping. One, two, three teachers stood around, attempting to herd the children together. Where was That Woman?

"How many are still inside?"

A red-haired woman, who emerged from the smoking doorway carrying the girl he'd talked to at the chicken coop the other day, coughed so hard she couldn't immediately reply. "I don't know. It is chaos! I tried to get the youngest, whose rooms are nearest to mine and instructed the older ones to follow me, but not everyone did." Her eyes filled with tears. "Half of them might still be inside."

This was a repeat of India. A repeat of his worst nightmare. People who died in front of him while he was doomed to look on helplessly. Marcus gritted his teeth. Well, not today. No one would die today. The devil was in it if he'd allow it to happen again.

"Stay outside and take care of the children," he ordered and walked into the inferno.

Smoke billowed into his face. He paused, turned to the windows, and pulled at the window drapes. Useless. The damask was too thick. His eyes flew frantically through the drawing room and paused at the table. He lifted the vase, yanked off the tablecloth, poured the water from the vase over the cloth and used that to press against his mouth and nose.

Then he dived deeper into the inferno.

There were still children inside. One came running toward him, one stood still, dazed, and one huddled in a corner, crying. He lifted one child, took the second one by the hand, and barked at the third to follow him. He ushered them out of the house and deposited them with the red-haired teacher.

He entered the building again and checked each room, flung open doors, and scanned each corner. One girl huddled in the bed, under her blankets, crying. He pulled her out and carried her outside.

Returning inside, he found two children in the library who attempted to escape through the window.

"Come with me. Put this over your mouths, and you'll be fine." He tossed the wet cloth at them and helped them outside.

"Count the children. How many are missing?" he barked at Miss Robinson.

"There are twenty here. We are twenty-five, not counting the teachers."

He nodded tersely and returned to the house.

The fire hadn't reached the lower floors yet. It was the roof and the upper rooms that were affected.

A maid stumbled down the stairs, wild-eyed. "You must get out! The roof is about to collapse!"

"How many up there?"

"I don't know." She shook her head.

He tore up the staircase, saw the doors to most rooms open and, thankfully, empty. Up to the higher floor.

There, the smoke was thicker and blacker. He dropped to his knees and crouched on the floor. Dropping the cloth he'd pressed over his nose, he bellowed at the top of his voice: "Is anyone still here?"

There was only the sound of flames and cracking wood.

Then he heard a muffled sound from one of the rooms. "In here!"

He rushed to the room.

Two girls huddled in a corner, crying.

The ceiling had already partially caved in, and a burning beam from the ceiling had crashed on a wardrobe, toppling it. Miss Hilversham knelt on the floor and tried to wrestle with the wardrobe. Her face was red as she tried, with all her strength, to move the heavy piece of furniture.

"She's trapped!"

A girl lay on the floor, her leg squeezed under the wardrobe. She was so pale and quiet that she appeared already dead.

With a rush of furious energy and a mighty roar, he lifted the wardrobe and shoved it aside with a crash. Miss Hilversham picked up the child.

The fire above them crackled and sizzled, and a second beam threatened to fall.

"Give her to me and take care of the others." He jerked his head towards the girls in the corner. Miss Hilversham placed the child in his arms. The girl hung limply, weighing no more than a feather.

"Get me a sheet from the bed." Miss Hilversham immediately understood his intentions. He tied the unconscious girl around his back, the way he'd seen Indian mothers carry their babies.

"Out!" he bellowed. "The roof's about to cave in."

They crawled on all fours, which was a challenge on the stairs. Smoke bit into their eyes, but somehow, they made it out. Teary, coughing, gasping, but alive.

"Is that all of them?"

"Twenty-five. All twenty-five children are here." The red-haired teacher sobbed with relief. Marcus passed the child he carried to her.

"Ellen, organise the children into groups. I will be with you in a minute." Miss Hilversham turned on her heels and promptly marched back into the burning house.

Marcus grabbed her by the arm. "Where do you think you are going?"

"Inside."

"The children are all out now, the servants and teachers as well."

"There is something I've forgotten." She shook her arm from his grasp and disappeared into the smoke. Calling a curse down on all mule-headed, opinionated schoolmistresses who refused to see reason, he went after her.

The house crackled, rumbled, and groaned about them. Rushing up the stairs, she tore the door open to one of the rooms, and a billow of smoke engulfed them.

She pounced on the commode and yanked open a drawer, pulled out an inlaid mahogany box and opened it with shaking hands. She secured a little velvet pouch in her décolleté.

Marcus could barely believe his eyes. "You are putting our lives in danger to get this—this thing?"

She whirled on him, and her eyes, bereft of spectacles, flashed. "You wouldn't understand this. It is worth putting my life in danger. And I never asked you to follow me, so it is entirely your fault if your life is in danger."

A pox on all females! He was about to retort that she was a blasted, bullheaded harridan whose sole existence in life seemed to be to pester him when suddenly the ceiling caved down on them.

He lunged forward and pushed her back. They crashed to the ground together, he on top of her, shielding her from the dust and bricks that came raining down with the burning wood.

This was it. Awareness that he was about to die hit him with full force and reflected in the huge, grey eyes that blinked back at him.

Who would've thought he would leave this world with

this shrew in his arms? He lay sprawled on top of her, and she looked up at him with wide, stunned eyes. If this had been any other situation, he might have been tempted to take advantage of the closeness of her lips; but they were unfortunately about to be roasted to toast, squashed to pancakes, and fried to cinders, and that knowledge dampened that growing feeling of…dash it all. Surely, it wasn't ardour?

He had no time to analyse this perplexing emotional state, for the woman began to struggle underneath him.

He scrambled off her, held out his hand to help her up, and surveyed the room. They were cut off from the door by the burning beam. He stared at the bed, which was still untouched, but not for long, for the fire was spreading rapidly.

He yanked the sheets and blankets off the bed.

"What are you doing?"

"Help me get the mattress. We need to get out of here."

"How?"

He pointed at the window. "Through here."

She understood immediately. Together, they heaved the mattress off the bed. She opened the window. "It's too small! It will never fit—" Marcus jumped onto the window ledge and kicked against the window frame, smashing the glass. The opening was now enough for the mattress to fit through diagonally. They shoved it out and let it fall to the ground with a thunk.

Marcus looked down and prayed it landed where he thought.

Behind them, the fire burned, and another beam threatened to fall.

"It's time to leave."

"It's too high." She looked down and hesitated.

Yes, it was a bit of a way down and one couldn't see the mattress, for it was dark, and whatever visibility there was was obscured by all the smoke.

"Woman. Make up your mind. Either we are to be squashed and fried if we stay up here—or we jump and have at least—" he squinted his eyes as he estimated, "a fifty-fifty chance of actually landing on the mattress and surviving, versus missing the mattress and getting our brains dashed out on the ground. Your choice." He motioned with his hand.

He'd evidently shocked her, for she stood frozen, and stared at him with a half-open mouth. Then she did something which shocked him.

She laughed.

It was a low, delighted, pleasant-sounding chuckle.

She was laughing? In the face of their deaths?

He'd expected tears and hysterics.

Had she gone mad?

"Thank you for being so honest and descriptive about the choice of our deaths." Her voice shook. "One thing is comforting. At least I won't die alone." She took his hand. "Shall we, Your Grace?"

He pulled her toward him, grabbed her by the waist, and pressed a hard kiss on her lips. Then, before either of them could change their minds, he hurled them out of the window.

Dropping through the air with a woman in his arms was a novel experience for him. At least he would die embracing a woman. He waited for the impact.

They landed with a thump in the middle of the

mattress. This time, she landed on top of him, squashing every ounce of breath out of his body.

"Well, we are still alive," Marcus noted thickly, as he untangled himself from her. In her attempt to scramble up, her elbow smashed into his stomach and swept her hair over his face. He blew the strands of fine hair out of his mouth.

He caught a whiff of lavender and lemon underneath the smoke. And there was more to her than sticks and bones. Beyond any doubt.

She held out her hand. He took it and scrambled up after her.

Ellen and Fariq came running towards them.

"You made it! I never thought I'd see you alive again," Ellen sobbed as she hugged Miss Hilversham.

"Flying through the window, I see," Fariq's voice wobbled in relief as he patted Marcus' shoulder. "No need to ask how you are, for I see you are indestructible."

"I must admit, I am rather glad to be on the outside of this furnace."

They watched in silence as the roof finally caved in on the room where they'd been standing only moments ago.

Fariq had organised a bucket brigade, leading right to the well in his garden, where everyone, even the littlest of students, participated, passing buckets of water to the next in line. The little lisping girl passed on a bucket that she could barely lift. The problem was that the fire was spreading too quickly, and it was like sprinkling drops of water onto an inferno.

"Is everyone out? Everyone alive?" Marcus shouted.

"All twenty-five students are out, only Emily is

injured," said Ellen. Emily was the girl who'd been buried under the wardrobe. "But she, too, will be fine."

"The teachers?"

"All here."

"Servants? Blast it, we forgot about the servants. They were probably sleeping right under the roof! They are probably dead by now. All dead. They cannot—she—must —not—be dead." The words came out in quick gasps. The inferno was all around him, the crumbled walls, the palm trees smashed, and one body on the ground right next to him. It had been so merry. The lampions lit up the sky, and strings of music drifted through the night. She'd been laughing, dancing, looking so happy, so alive. Then the jaws of hell had opened, literally, right under his feet, with a shaking and a roaring and a rumbling, and he found himself thrown against a wall. Dazed, he scrambled up. Where was she? He stumbled through the rubble, sifted stones, and bodies, covered by ash and dust, surrounded by death. The fire roared and licked up the remains, like the jaws of hell.

"Must find her...Adika!" She was likely inside, buried under the rubble. He turned to stride right back into the burning blaze when someone pulled him back.

"Your Grace!" A tug of his hand. Insistent, hard. "Everyone is out. The servants are here. Only Emily is hurt, but she's woken in the meantime and her foot is broken. No one is dead. Do you hear?"

He blinked, dazed, and looked down.

His hand was interlaced with a female one, fine and white. Her other hand grabbed his shoulder.

Ever since they'd fallen out of the window, the woman had never let go of his hand.

"You got everyone out in time. Everyone is safe. You are a hero."

"Everyone is safe," he echoed dumbly. "No one is dead?"

"No one. Who is Adika? You said you must find her. Was she inside?"

His vision focused on the woman beside him, and he returned to the present. This was not India. This was not an earthquake. This was an inferno, all right, but she said that everyone was safe.

He looked at her with disbelief. "But everyone died." He said, hoarsely. "Everyone except me and Pen."

A look of understanding entered her grey eyes. "Penelope told me about it. The earthquake that killed her parents. It was tragic. This here--" she waved her free hand at the house. A brigade of firemen had arrived and pumped water at the fire. "This is also tragic. But no lives are lost. Thankfully. Thanks to you. You have saved our lives. Please don't go dashing back into the burning house. I know what I did was foolish, so please don't imitate me. There is no point at all, other than getting yourself killed, and then you will have, in addition to hero status, acquired a martyr status, and then we shall be forced to rename the school after you, in commemoration. *The Duke of Rochford's Establishment for Young Ladies.* Appalling. Wouldn't you agree?" A smile darted over her face.

He blinked. "Indeed. Somehow, that doesn't sound right."

"No, it doesn't in the least." Her eyes surveyed the scene and sadness fell over them.

A group of men pumped the handle of a water engine, while another held the leather hose and directed the water jet at the fire. Fariq's bucket brigade continued throwing water as well. The entire neighbourhood had assembled, many merely to watch, while others came to offer help.

"I should probably help them put out the fire," Marcus attempted to remove his hand, but she held on tight.

"No," she replied. "You did enough. Give others the chance to be heroic, too." She shook her head. "It was incredible. You—were incredible. A real hero."

"I am not a hero," he snapped.

She patted his hand maternally. She would have patted his cheek if he had let her. "I am afraid you are. You saved most of the pupils in the school. Including myself. If you hadn't come along when the wardrobe jammed Emily's foot…." Her voice petered off.

"You would have stayed in there with the children," he said harshly. "And then you went right back inside again for what, exactly?"

She pulled out her trinket. "This. Don't you dare reprimand me. Some things are worth dying for."

He stared at the little lock of hair on her hand.

His hand involuntarily went to his pocket, where he was carrying Adika's miniature.

Unthinkable if he'd ever lost it. He supposed he would've acted the same as her.

He nodded his head jerkily. "I understand."

CHAPTER THIRTEEN

Tragic Fire

Renowned Girls School burns to the ground. Casualties unknown.

'Disaster' was not an appropriate word to describe the entire scope of the situation. For some things in life, there were simply no words. Eleonore could not pinpoint the emotions that rushed through her after the paralysing numbness lifted. Dejection, anguish, grief, anxiety, followed by relief. For it could have been worse, much worse.

Some events in life were like sharp-edged corners one had to get around; razor-sharp blades that cut one open and tore out one's insides, but one had to move around them somehow because that was how life worked.

She'd encountered many such edges in her life, and she'd pulled herself up again and again every time, gritted her teeth and dragged herself on, one foot in front of the other.

The burning of her beloved school was yet another edge.

Her entire existence had burned to rubble.

Her income, her identity, her dreams, her future—all gone.

How was she to get around this edge? She had no strength left anymore. She was tired. So, so tired.

Eleonore was still wearing her nightgown from the night of the fire, for she had nothing else to wear. She'd risen early and padded out of the duke's house, with naked feet, to the smoking remains of her school.

Only the blackened façade remained, with empty holes where the windows used to be. Amid the rubble, she could identify what once had been a piano. The remaining furniture had burned to cinders.

The library! All the books!

If she could weep, she would, but the numbness had taken over again and held her tightly.

It felt entirely unreal as if she were trapped in a nightmare.

All the strength left her. She dropped onto the grass and wrapped her arms around her legs.

After the fire had been put out, several neighbours had stepped forward to offer them housing. Some suggested dividing up the children, with each neighbour taking in two or three. Mrs Benningfield, who lived in a large mansion on a sweeping estate not too far away, said this was nonsense. They should all stay with her until a more permanent solution was found.

But then the duke had spoken up in his curt voice that they would all stay in his house, period. "All we need are additional blankets, mattresses and pillows."

And maybe because he was a duke, or maybe because of his imperious way that did not allow any contradiction, people immediately agreed and willingly supplied not only the requested bedding but also food. Loads of food. They brought bread, seed cakes, biscuits, sausages, pots of soup, pies, meat patties and puddings, and more.

"Miss Hilversham." The duke turned to her. "We have seven rooms in the house. Divide everyone into groups and Fariq will assign them each to a room." He pointed at Emily. "Take the injured child, together with that one," he pointed down at his side, where May clung, "to the master bedroom. The rest distribute in the remaining rooms." He bent down to scoop up Emily, who smiled at him wanly.

Then Eleonore became aware that her leadership skills had been sadly lacking.

She gathered all the children and ordered everyone to be sorted into groups, each accompanied by a teacher.

"Children. We are to be guests at the duke's house, so behave accordingly. I want to thank each of you for being the reasonable, well-mannered ladies that we have raised you to be. This situation isn't easy for anyone." She swallowed before she continued, "least of all for the youngest amongst us. It is uncertain how this situation will continue. Life always has uncertainties in store for us, unexpected events, tragedies." She paused for a moment. "It is the way it is. We can but take each moment in time, and despite this disaster, I am profoundly grateful that you are—mostly—unharmed. Things could have been so much worse." Her voice shook with emotion. "Rest assured, I will contact your parents and guardians to discuss the next proceedings. And now, go to your rooms. Mr Fariq will show you where." She gestured at Fariq, who ushered the children upstairs.

The duke gave a curt nod of approval and left.

She was sharing his bedroom with Emily and May. The doctor had splinted and bandaged Emily's foot, and while the girl had cried for a while, she had calmed down and fallen asleep. Eleonore had slept next to her on the big bed, with May on the other side. She was strangely aware that she was lying on his bed. Where he'd been sleeping before the fire had awoken him. It was oddly intimate. And comforting.

Exhausted, she'd fallen asleep, only to wake up every hour. At one point, May had disappeared from the bed. Eleonore had taken the candle, left the bedroom, and checked on all the other children.

In the drawing room, she found the men expired on the sofas. Fariq's long legs dangled over the armrest, and his arms grazed the floor, his mouth was open.

On the other sofa slept the duke. He lay sideways and curled under the nook of his arm was—May. She snuggled up to him, her thumb in her mouth, soundly asleep.

The sight of the two touched Eleonore. Both were outsiders, lost souls. She wondered whether the duke knew May was deaf, which was why she spoke oddly. The little girl had taken a liking to the duke, that was clear.

She stared at the face of the sleeping duke.

He was frowning even in his sleep, his thick, black eyebrows drawn together. His lips were firm, sensual and slightly parted.

It was strange, she thought, how differently she thought of him now.

Yesterday she hated him with a passion. She saw him

as nothing but a degenerate philanderer, which he no doubt was.

How could she have known that behind that façade was one of the most courageous men she'd ever met, one who was so selfless in his desire to help others, one who did not shy away from danger and the loss of his own life? A duke who gave up his bed for a wounded child and her teacher. It was not only selfless…it was kind.

Heroic. Selfless, kind. She almost snorted. These were not words she thought she'd ever attribute to him.

Had those signs always been there? Or had she simply been blind, driven by prejudice?

She reached out, and her fingers hovered over his forehead.

He shifted in his sleep and groaned. She pulled her fingers back.

He was plagued by demons. And his nights, too, were restless and full of nightmares.

Since everyone had been sleeping, she had gone out, and this is where she was now, sitting on the grass, staring at her former home. Grey stripes of dawn crept over the horizon, and the acrid smell of the fire still lingered in the air.

Eleonore had to force herself out of this paralysis. She had to do something. She had to decide upon the next course of action.

Write to the parents. Have them collect the children. But what about the children who did not have anyone? Little May, for one. Her guardian never wrote. What about the teachers who considered the seminary their home? Like Ellen. Where would they go?

What about rebuilding the school? Was it worth

reviving this ruin? What about her dreams of expanding it, of acquiring the neighbouring estate? She would now have to use the funds she'd saved for renovation. Would her patrons keep on supporting her? Or would they withdraw their children from the seminary?

So many questions. So many problems.

She rubbed the space between her brows wearily.

She heard footsteps shuffling in the grass beside her and someone dropped heavily next to her. She did not have to turn her head to know it was the duke. He, too, was barefoot. He crossed his legs and stared morosely at the burned-down building.

They sat in silence, staring at the wreckage.

It was oddly companionable.

"There will have to be an investigation into how the fire was started," he eventually said.

She felt hot tears rush into her eyes. "It was Martha. She swears it was an accident. I believe her." Martha had come to her, sobbing, confessing that she had fallen asleep over a book, and she'd left the candle burning. She had been trying to teach herself to read. But she'd been tired. It had been a long day, and she'd merely closed her eyes for a second...

"You will have to dismiss her."

"No." Eleonore shook her head decisively. "I can't do that. She will never find another position. She would end up in the streets and I won't allow that."

He studied her face. "It appears Miss Hilversham has a soft heart for her servants."

"Martha belongs to us like everyone else. She is family. She made a mistake, but I won't have her cast out. I don't want an investigation." She rubbed her eyebrow and swallowed the tears away. With an investigation, the school's meticulous reputation would be gone for good. "This is the end," she whispered.

He threw her a surprised look. "Come now. Never tell me you're giving up that easily. The spitfire hellcat priggish schoolmistress? Where has her spirit gone? I'm disappointed."

She smiled wanly. "I am trying to be realistic. My pupils come from the best houses in England. Dukes, earls, viscounts. They all send their daughters and wards to me so I can give them a modern education without neglecting the traditional values in which they were raised, and the expectations they are eventually to fulfil."

"What expectations?"

"To haul in a husband, of course. Preferably one with a title." She lifted an eyebrow ironically. "Preferably a duke."

"Ah. Of course. Silly of me to have forgotten."

"So, the implicit understanding was that I would raise them to be well-educated women who are also fit for the marriage market. They entrusted their daughters to me because it was understood that I would care for them and that they would be safe. Physically, and of course morally, safe. Meaning that the immediate vicinity of the school is safe for them as well." She sent him a sidelong glance.

"Ah." He scratched the back of his neck. "Who would've known The Wicked Duke would come along and set up a gaming hell right next door, endangering their moral, er, ah, safety, as you put it? What is it you called it? A 'den of iniquity.'"

"I see we understand each other perfectly."

"Continue."

"Well, it turns out they made a mistake. Miss Hilversham failed miserably in keeping them safe. They all nearly died in last night's fire." She swallowed. "She not only failed in keeping her children safe, she, herself, had to be saved." She shook her head as if she still could not believe it. "In the face of all this, I wouldn't mind in the least if you were to set up ten gaming clubs in the area if only it would've prevented the school from burning down. I can't even think of the implications of what could've happened." Her voice wobbled and her hand shook as she angrily swiped away a strand of hair that had fallen into her face. "I let them all down."

"This is a bag full of moonshine. None of this is your fault. So don't you take on any responsibility for this."

"Why are you suddenly being so nice?" she blurted out. "Saving us. Our school. Offering us accommodation. Finding the right words of comfort. You could've left us out in the cold. Triumphed over our demise."

"You didn't have to take up my offer, did you? You could have slept in a more comfortable bed in Mrs Benningfield's mansion," he reminded her.

"Your bed was comfortable, and I enjoyed sleeping there." She clasped her hand across her mouth. "I can't believe I just said that."

He threw his head back and laughed. He had a pleasant laugh, deep and rumbly, and a bit rusty, as though he didn't laugh too often.

"To answer your question. I am not nice. I am revelling in a victor's joy that his foe is forevermore squelched. The object of opposition is overcome. I have triumphed." He stretched his arms in front, intertwined his fingers, and cracked his knuckles. "Why don't you sell me this pile of stone and ash? I will build up the biggest gambling hell

England has ever seen, and you will have enough money to, I don't know," he waved his hand about, "buy another pretty house elsewhere and continue your school."

"Be quiet," she said, crossly. "You don't mean any of this. I suspect you never did." She was beginning to know him rather well now, wasn't she?

He was indeed quiet for a moment as he surveyed the smoking disaster in front of them. "It will take a good amount of blunt to resurrect this. And some diplomacy to convince the high sticklers to keep sending their children here. Who are your patrons?"

"Threthewick. Dunross. The Earl of Halsford himself painted the mural. Did you know he is the painter Tiverton? His wife was a teacher here." She had to blink again heavily, for the thought of the loss of the mural pained her. "And, of course, the Duke of Ashmore."

Marcus snorted. "Congratulations. You've gathered the highest, proudest, starchiest of the lot. Unforgivable pricks, all of them, especially Ashmore. Of course, they will all withdraw their children now."

She plucked out a handful of grass. "Their patronage is because their wives were students here. Their children are not attending school yet, since they are but infants, but that is a moot point as there is no school."

"So, talk with them. Convince them to open their pockets for more blunt."

Her shoulders slumped. She stared at the sooty house in front of her. Her eyes burned with unshed tears. She would have to start all over again.

Maybe he was right. Maybe she should sell it to him.

And she, unencumbered, could finally do what she wanted: travel the world and disappear.

Instead, she changed the subject. "And Little May? Is she back in her room?"

He shook his head. "I put her down on the sofa, and she slept so deeply she did not wake up."

"She seems oddly taken with you."

"What can I say but women like me?" He flashed his teeth at her. "It is a curse I cannot seem to shake."

She leaned her chin on her knees as she studied him.

"Yesterday, you were about to throw yourself into the burning house again because you thought someone else was still inside." Maybe that was too personal, and she expected him to rebuff her.

To her surprise, he pulled out a silver locket, opened it, and, after some hesitation, showed it to her.

She gasped. "It's Penelope!" Then she took another look. She wasn't wearing her spectacles, so she squinted her eyes together. The dark-haired woman in the painting with the big, dark eyes and half-smile looked young and sweet. Her face was innocent, her eyes cheerful.

"Not quite."

"Pen's mother," she whispered.

So that was how matters stood.

He clasped the locket shut and pocketed it again. "She died in that earthquake. I couldn't save her. I tried so hard, but she, and John," he swallowed, "I found them under the rubble. Everything was burning, too. I tried so hard to find someone who'd survived, and for the longest time I thought no one did, that I was the only one."

"But then you found Pen," she whispered.

He nodded. "You see, I consider myself responsible." He stared empty-eyed into the distance. "So, I know all about that feeling. It poisons you slowly."

"But why?"

"Because the entire affair had been my idea," he said savagely. "If I hadn't insisted on this infernal ball, they might still be alive today. They wanted to travel, but I, idiot that I am, suggested throwing a farewell ball and inviting half the village. I organised it all. Everyone who came, except for me and Pen, ended up dead. I have this morbid speciality, you know, that all people I care for die. If they'd just stuck to their original plans and travelled when they said they wanted to, they'd still be alive today." He said savagely. "I never wanted to tell you any of this. Why am I saying this at all? To you of all people. The point I am trying to make, I suppose, is that I deserve every bit of my reputation. I am personally responsible for the deaths of many, many people. I am haunted by it every single waking moment. I revisit it, night by night, and every time it is the same. I try to save them. I run while everything shakes and burns. But I am always too late." His voice shook. "It is all my fault."

Eleonore sat up. "What is this nonsense, Your Grace? You are being as arrogant as always. By all things that are right and good, but you are not responsible for the forces of nature. You are not God."

He blinked at her. "But—"

"Be quiet. Now I am talking." She knew she was as schoolmistress-ish as ever, but she could not help herself. "Neither are you responsible for the fates, lives, and deaths of other people. The only thing you are responsible for is excess, but organising a farewell party for your friends and making merry before they leave on a voyage is hardly excess. It is what any good friend would do. So, I suggest you stop carrying a burden that was never yours to carry. It was not your fault. And ultimately," she shrugged, "as terrible as it sounds, we all must die. It is a fact of life."

He looked at her as if a thunderbolt had stricken him from the sky. "Can you repeat that?"

"Which part would you like me to repeat? I think the point of my speech is simply this: it isn't your fault. None of it was." She spoke gentler, kinder.

He leaned his forehead against his pulled up knees. His shoulders shook.

Eleonore sat quietly next to him and hardly dared to breathe. She did not touch him. She did not say a word. The silence between them was healing, calming as if the deep rift that had been between them had mended.

When he looked up, his face was wet.

Lucky him, Eleonore thought, that he could cry where she couldn't.

After a while, her foot cramped, and her stomach growled.

"I suppose I will have to go back inside and be the leader everyone expects me to be and start solving everyone's problems." She wanted to sound her factual, cool self, but it sounded more forlorn than she intended.

A hand fell over hers, big and strong, with a crushing grip. "You are not alone. I promise."

CHAPTER FOURTEEN

Heroic duke
single-handedly saves 30 people from fire

*A*fter they returned to the house, they saw that Fariq had taken over command. He'd arranged for everyone to be seated at tables, or any object that could function as a table, and everyone was quietly eating breakfast.

The clattering of the plates, the munching and sipping, stopped when Marcus and Eleonore entered. Twenty-five shiny faces turned towards them, focusing on Marcus.

"What?" He rubbed his jaw. Eleonore understood, with a tinge of amusement, that he did this, in addition to drawing his eyebrows into a ferocious scowl, whenever he felt put on the spot.

Little May stepped up to him and pulled at his sleeve. "You're a hero. My hero."

Twenty-five heads nodded, hero-worship glistened in their eyes.

He took a step back.

Ellen got up and folded her hands. "May is right. The children and I, and all the teachers and servants of Miss Hilversham's seminary, would like to thank you for saving our lives."

"Nonsense." He attempted to lift his hands to ward them off, but Little May held onto him, so he was forced to hold her hand instead.

Eleonore stepped up. "Ellen and the children are quite right. We haven't properly thanked you. We are deep in your debt, Your Grace."

"What is this nonsense?" he growled.

Little May dropped to the floor and pulled him down to a makeshift table, which consisted of a box covered with a tablecloth. He sat down next to her on the floor, cross-legged, and inquired what she was eating.

"The betht breakfatht ever," she announced.

Indeed, the neighbours had delivered plenty of cornbread, butter, and jam, and the cook had brewed gallons of tea and coffee.

A maid handed Eleonore a cup of coffee, which she sipped gratefully.

"What are we to do today, Miss Hilversham?" a tall, brown-haired girl asked. She was one of the older students and had been taking care of a group of younger ones. "We can hardly have classes today, can we?"

All eyes turned to her. Once more, the feeling of being overwhelmed engulfed her. Decisions! She had to make decisions. Her mind drew a blank, and her chest constricted tightly: panic.

Her eyes wandered around and fell on the duke.

He set down his cup. "Of course, you will have classes. How can something as paltry as having your school burned down keep you from learning? That is after you have helped clear up the breakfast dishes—you and you —" he pointed at Annabelle and Rosemary, "and you two here," he pointed at two little ones who were still eating, "are going to help Fariq organise papers, pencils and quills. There ought to be some of that stuff lying about in this house somewhere, I suppose. If there isn't enough, you will knock on the neighbour's door—that woman yesterday with the massive bosom and the shrill voice. What was her name?"

Some teachers gasped, but the children erupted in delighted giggles.

"Mrs Benningfield," they answered in a chorus.

"You will go ask her for whatever supplies you need; I daresay she has aplenty. And the teachers, where are the teachers?" Ellen and her colleagues raised their hands. "Organise the day into the usual schedule. There is no reason they shouldn't learn composition and arithmetic and whatever else it is you normally teach this brood."

Eleonore nodded. "I will inform the teachers who do not stay with us at the boarding school because they come from the outside that they are to hold their classes at their usual hours. Instead of the seminary, they are to come here. We will create makeshift classrooms."

"We want another lesson on Indian history, Your Grace!" Annabelle piped up.

Marcus warded her off. "Your man for that would be Fariq. He knows so much more about this topic than I."

All eyes turned to Fariq, who assumed an expression of horror. "Blimey. Me? Teach?"

"Best teacher in town." Marcus slapped Fariq's shoulder.

It was unusual for Eleonore not to be in charge. But for the first time in her life, she was glad that someone else was.

"And you," the duke turned to her. "You will sit down immediately and write letters. You may use my study."

She nodded. Of course. It was the most sensible thing to do.

After everyone was busy, each child assigned to a task, Eleonore marvelled at how they were now at the mercy of the duke, and how, not three days ago, she would've been utterly horrified to know she'd gladly let the duke make decisions for her. What was even odder was that they seemed to be getting along rather well.

He wasn't half as bad a man as she originally thought him to be. He was just—a bit like a layered onion, she supposed. She happened to like onions.

She was glad that he reminded her, in a very logical, practical manner, of what had to be done. Everyone looked to him for guidance, and she was glad to be away, for once, from the limelight. The shock still sat deep, and her brain still didn't seem to function as usual.

With a sigh, she picked up the quill and wrote a letter to the first parent. How on earth did one write such a letter? *It is with great regret that I have to inform you that our school burned down, and your child nearly died...*

She sighed again.

Then she steeled herself. It had to be done.

THE WEEKS PASSED, AND THEY WERE STILL LIVING AT THE duke's house. In the meantime, most pupils had been picked up by their parents or guardians, and only a few remained, such as Little May. Of the teachers, only Ellen remained.

With the duke's help, the workers had set immediately to work clearing up the rubble. The outer, hollow shell of her former school looked woefully empty, and every time Eleonore looked at it, her heart squeezed.

"What is to be done?" she kept asking herself. What would become of her? Of the school?

She could not find the answer.

SUMMER WAS ALMOST OVER, AND AUTUMN HAD MOVED INTO the country. The nights were cool and the days were rainy. His house gradually emptied itself of the students, the noise, and the controlled chaos. It was odd how fast he'd got used to it.

Marcus had found it interesting to observe how the teachers taught, and how they interacted with the students, including Miss Hilversham, who was a born teacher and truly wonderful with the children. She was more than a teacher, he realised. She was almost like a mother to them.

Fariq had become a prime favourite with the children. He'd taught them all about Indian history. Never mind that most of it were anecdotes and fairy tales. The children adored it. He played cricket outside and taught them how to play piquet. The teachers turned a blind eye every time he pulled out his pack of cards. To Marcus's great amusement, the older girls were all in love with Fariq, and the younger ones saw him as their playmate. As for himself, he'd been placed on an uncomfortably high pedestal: that of a hero. They painted watercolour pictures of him on a white horse, saving them all. One of them even bound a wreath of laurel and attempted to press it onto his head. That had been too much for him, and he'd fled.

Even the newspapers picked up on this ridiculous story of his heroism. He could barely open a newspaper these days without finding a reference to him and the role he'd played in saving so many lives.

Marcus noticed that Miss Hilversham withdrew more and more as the days passed. There was frequently a blank look on her face when people addressed her.

She seemed to sleep as little as he. One night, he caught her slipping out of the house, wrapped only in a shawl. What was that woman doing? He followed her from a distance. She went to the burned-out house, staring at it for a while. She went further back and stopped by the well, peering down. He saw how she braced her two arms against the brim as if to haul herself up.

What the deuce was she doing?

He rushed up and gripped her arm. "Don't fall in," he growled.

She started and pressed a hand over her heart. "Goodness me," she said breathlessly, "you scared me."

"It looked like you were about to drown yourself."

"I–I" she shook her head. "Of course not. I just wanted to see the bottom of the well."

"Rather difficult to do in this darkness. And the lamp

you brought with you isn't likely to give much light, either."

She sighed. "I suppose not. It's just that I couldn't sleep."

"So, you tend to walk about at night when you can't sleep?"

"The truth is that I threw a coin." She looked down the well. "It's a wishing well and they say one is supposed to throw in coins at midnight." She smiled. "I have it on good authority that it fulfils everyone's wishes."

"Does it, indeed?" He looked down into the water. It was oily black, and only the moon and the stars reflected in it. "I suppose it can't harm."

"No, it can't."

They looked at each other, and suddenly the atmosphere between them changed. The air, heavy with their silence, tingled with something that hadn't been there before. She seemed to feel it too, for she blushed, looked away, and fiddled around with the edge of her shawl.

He took an involuntary step closer.

She looked up. There was such vulnerability in her eyes, a melancholy, a sadness, a desire, that he caught his breath. She smelled of lavender and lemon, and she was a woman, all woman.

The first kiss he'd given her hadn't counted. He'd done it mainly to provoke her. This time, he really wanted to kiss her. Properly. Thoroughly. Make her his. He wanted to answer the silent question in her eyes, in the only way he knew how.

He pulled her into his arms and kissed her deeply,

with aching neediness that he had never felt before. He kissed her like a woman ought to be kissed.

And it was good.

She melted into him and responded with a passion that left him breathless.

He released her, gently. Her hand went to her mouth as if in wonder.

His heart hammered irregularly. Would she slap him again?

"Thank you," she whispered. This almost floored him.

He grabbed the edge of the well to stabilise himself.

"You have given me hope. And also..." she hesitated. "I had forgotten what it was like." She placed her hand against his stubbled cheek. Then she drifted away like a ghost, and he was alone beside the well, staring after her in stupefaction.

Something had changed. Something monumental had shifted, and it wasn't without, but within. She'd touched him somehow. Not on the cheek, though her touch still burned there even though her hand had been cool.

What the devil had happened just now?

Why was he feeling this disturbing, oozy sensation around where his heart was supposed to be?

He hadn't been aware of the location of this particular organ in, oh, more than a decade, maybe even two. He'd all but forgotten he even had one.

And now, one kiss made him aware that he had a heart?

What was all this talk about the heart, anyhow?

That look in her eyes, by George.

He felt profoundly disturbed.

It was just a kiss. He'd kissed many women. It did not signify. It was what he did. It was what he enjoyed doing.

But the look in her eyes just now. The entire world had been in them. A dawning hope.

He pulled his hands through his thick hair.

Hope?

Hope for what?

Certainly not love.

Sweet Jupiter.

That would never happen. It simply could not happen, only over the corpse of his nonexistent heart.

He knew all about love. It started subtly, with hope. It crept up on you gingerly, slowly. And when you were least aware of it, in a perfectly innocuous moment, it pounced, and you would awaken one morning and find yourself in love.

One couldn't get rid of it, ever. No matter how inconvenient, how forbidden. How impossible.

It would eat its way through all organs, possess one's brains, and seep into the blood, more toxic than opium, and all one could think of was her, exist only for her, every breath would be for her and her alone.

He groaned.

Yes, he knew all about love.

It brought pain and destruction, and a yearning that was never, ever fulfilled. And he wanted nothing to do with it.

His steps quickened to a run.

He would have to leave immediately.

Anywhere but here, away from her.

Away from the power of love.

CHAPTER FIFTEEN

Wicked Duke or Hero?

Ladies, rejoice! The Duke of R has been seen in London. With the season about to start, this is excellent news for our marriage mart. Regardless of whether he is a scoundrel or hero, it is generally agreed upon that This Duke is The Prime catch of the season...

"What do you mean, he is gone?" Eleonore thought she'd misheard.

"He left while everyone was sleeping, ma'am." Fariq was packing a trunk in his bedroom.

The Duke of Rochford had left early in the morning, without saying goodbye to anyone, Fariq included. Fariq seemed to take it with equanimity as he merely shrugged and mentioned that "His Grace has the unfortunate tendency to disappear without a word whenever he sees fit."

"And how long does it take him to appear again?" Eleonore asked with some foreboding.

Fariq scratched his neck. "It could take some years if he takes himself off to India or the West Indies."

Eleonore felt an involuntary pang. "India! The West Indies? Surely not?"

"He talked about that before he got all entangled in this," he waved his hand about. "It's somewhat inconvenient, I must add. I, myself, have a club to run in London and cannot take care of his affairs here in Bath forever." He threw a hopeful look at Eleonore. "But you are eager to rent this house at a cheap price, yes? I can offer a symbolic price even. For a penny a month."

"Are you telling me you want us to stay here?"

"Of course. I can also shut the house down again or resell it, but if you are going to stay here, it would be better. A house needs people in it. Especially after we just renovated it. Also, someone needs to take care of all the art." He lifted an Indian statue that stood by the bedside. "Everyone would benefit. What are your plans?"

Eleonore sighed. "I can hardly reopen the school here for the next term."

Ellen Robinson, who had been looking for Eleonore and listened to part of their conversation, leaned against the doorway with crossed her arms. "Why not?"

"As kind and generous and supportive as His Grace and Fariq here have been, and as much as we appreciate their help, surely you agree that this is hardly a place for setting up a school?"

"Aside from the fact that we lack the necessary furniture, the desks and pulpit and several blackboards, why not?" Ellen countered. "This house is even bigger than our old schoolhouse, and there is enough space for bedrooms. It would be a good transition while the school building is being repaired."

Eleonore massaged her temples. "You may be right." She turned to Fariq. "Are you certain the duke will not mind? He left so quickly there was no time to discuss this. Besides, I thought the whole conflict was about him not wanting to give up this house to us. Now, it appears he has us as permanent residents here. What do you think brought about this change of mind?"

"Boredom." Fariq folded a scarf and placed it into the trunk. "His Grace has left his entire affairs in my capable hands. Rest assured, he won't care what happens to this house."

"Then why not just sell it to us?"

"I believe that is the only limitation he's put on me. Do whatever you want here. But the house is to remain mine." He imitated the duke's cadence.

"It's not too bad, is it?" Ellen, forevermore the optimist, said. "We can rent the house and stay here until the school is rebuilt. What other option do we have?"

Ellen was right.

"I will have to make a trip to London myself to talk to the solicitors." She would also have to visit the patrons, explain her situation, and ask for more funds. It was as awkward as it could get. Then there was another very personal reason she needed to be in London. But she kept that reason to herself.

"When are you leaving?" Ellen asked.

"As soon as possible. I trust I can leave everything in your capable hands here? Unless you, too, would like to take leave."

Ellen shook her head. "You need me here. Besides, there is nowhere else to go, and Little May also needs me."

Eleonore nodded.

Fariq closed his trunk and lifted it from the bed. "Well, ladies, Miss Hilversham, if I can give you a ride to London, you have but say the word."

"When are you leaving?"

"Tomorrow morning, at the first shriek of the rooster."

James, the rooster, had, of course, survived the fiasco unscathed and kept on crowing to his heart's content.

Eleonore wrestled with herself before replying, "Very well. I will join you."

FARIQ SET HER DOWN IN FRONT OF A TOWNHOUSE IN Berkeley Square, and she stared at the white house with the iron fence in front. It had been her godmother's. The house was hers now, but it had been standing empty all this time. As she placed the key in the keyhole, she hesitated. Entering this house meant unrolling the past again. Stepping through this door meant opening a chapter she had long closed. Maybe it was better to stay in Grillon's hotel. But they would frown upon a single woman like her, for she had brought no companion, and she was not interested in having to convince anyone to rent her a room elsewhere. Seen in this light, her godmother's old townhouse was golden. She hesitated one moment longer, then turned the key. The door opened with a creak.

Sunlight poured through the grime-covered windows, illuminating the cobwebs that hung in the corners like wisps of lace. The furniture was draped with holland covers, and the carpets were rolled up. There were no servants to greet her. No fire warmed the fireplace, and there would be no hot cup of tea waiting for her. The house was barren and cold.

She looked with a whiff of melancholy up the stair-case, expecting her godmother to appear any moment. She'd been a robust woman even in her late seventies, who had not remarried after her husband died early, and yet she had lived an independent, full life.

"One doesn't need a man to be happy, Violetta," she'd always told her.

Eleonore thought she'd agreed with her, only to fall in love with the first man who'd crossed her path.

She hadn't thought of Edward in such a long time. But now that she stood in the foyer of her godmother's house, the memories flooded back. She closed her eyes painfully.

Her godmother, Lady Madelyn Adkins, had been an eccentric. She ran one of the most popular literary salons where artists, writers and intellectuals gathered to converse and debate on intellectual topics. Eleonore was encouraged to attend as well, even though she was not considered officially "out" yet. Thus, it came to be that whatever education she'd lacked as a child, she made up quickly under her aunt's tutelage and literary circles. Her aunt's library was stuffed with books, and Eleonore was encouraged to read to her heart's content.

The library! With a pounding heart, Eleonore stepped to the white door, now grey with dust, and opened it. It was dark and musty inside.

But she could smell it, the old books, paper, and dust. Eleonore crossed the room to open the shutters and allow sunshine and fresh air to flood into the room.

Here, she'd met and discussed poetry with the great

William Wordsworth. She discussed social reform with a peculiar young baron who was wild and moody, but passionate about his political views. He limped but was wonderfully beautiful to behold as passion shone in his dark eyes. He charmed all females. He told her about his poems, and that he intended to be very famous one day.

"What is your opinion on the matter, young lady?" he kept asking her, flattering her thoroughly. She'd not yet been seventeen.

She hadn't fallen in love with Byron, no.

She'd fallen for his friend instead.

Edward Lawrence, with the easy-going smile, the reckless impishness that lurked in his mud-brown eyes. She hadn't realised then that his charm was easily bestowed on anyone, and that his smile was cold and did not reflect what was in his heart.

It had been easy for him to seduce her, for she had been an innocent.

Eleonore looked around, and it was as if she could still see both men there, leaning nonchalantly against the fire-place, passionately discussing poetry and politics.

She'd been so happy then.

Eleonore wiped a strand of hair from her face and sighed as she surveyed the room.

It would be a tremendous amount of work to clean up this place. Was it worth it for the few days she intended to stay here? Maybe it was best to leave the library closed and not meddle with the past.

She went upstairs and aired the bed. She shook out the sheets, which were thankfully dry and not mildewy, and there was a vague whiff of lavender in the air, for Aunt

Madelyn's maid had stuffed all the drawers with lavender pouches.

Her stomach grumbled.

There would be nothing in the kitchen, but she'd brought some food with her, some apples, bread and cheese. With some foresight, Martha had packed her a small satchel of tea as well. She blessed Martha now. After the accident with the fire, she had been inconsolable. Poor girl.

Eleonore would make a fire on the stove and boil some tea.

The memory of the duke came up, of how he'd made tea for her. Masala chai. An involuntary smile passed over her face.

As she boiled water in the kitchen and became more aware than ever that she was alone in the house, a feeling of homesickness flooded over her with such violence that she sat down in the chair.

Homesickness for Martha, Ellen, and all her students.

For the school.

Her home.

Her world.

Her chest clenched together as if someone squeezed it with an iron fist.

Why couldn't she cry?

She pulled out her trinket, which she always carried with her.

She counted the days.

August fifteenth. In three days.

She clenched her fingers around it.

There was much to do for her school, and people to

talk to, but there was one important thing she had to do first.

Her fingers shook as she poured the boiling water into her mug.

It would take all her courage; she would have to do this with the entire strength of her soul. No one who knew her as Miss Hilversham, the fearless, strict, prim headmistress of the school, would believe she could be reduced to this bundle of nerves.

Eleonore Hilversham, afraid of something?

What would the world come to?

A hollow thumping rang through the house.

Eleonore nearly dropped her mug. Her heart rattled against her ribcage.

Who could it be?

Should she ignore it?

Yet again, someone was hammering insistently on the brass knocker.

She got up, brushed down her skirt, and stepped swiftly up the stairs into the hallway leading to the front door.

Again, the knock.

With a big breath, she opened the door.

A woman with a gigantic feathered hat stood outside. "Ah! I knew I didn't imagine it! There is someone here, after all! Oh! But I know you! Let me see. Were you not Madelyn's relative? Her ward?" The woman had a shrill, curious voice.

It was a long time ago, but Eleonore recognised her.

"Good day, Mrs Glissing." She lived next door. Mrs Glissing was not only her godmother's neighbour, but had also been a close friend.

"Violetta!"

Eleonore closed her eyes for two seconds.

"How wonderful that you have returned!" The woman attempted to look past her into the hallway. "I saw that someone arrived, and I could not help but wonder, you see. Knowing your aunt passed away so long ago."

"I am merely in town for several days; I have not returned for good." Eleonore gripped the door. "You must forgive me. I would ask you inside, but as you can see, the entire place is uninhabitable and rather dusty."

"Yes, yes, it hasn't been cleaned in quite a while. It must be in a terrible state. No matter! Have you found someone yet?"

Eleonore shook her head. "I have just arrived."

"Have you, indeed? I know just the right person for you. Betty's sister wanted to get into service. Betty being my current abigail, you know."

"I don't intend to hire anyone—" Eleonore started, but Mrs Glissing interrupted her.

"Nonsense, of course you need someone. You can't live in this hovel all on your own. Ah, what a place this used to be. How well I remember when Madelyn was still alive. It was such a vibrant place, was it not? Nightly soirees and circles, as she called them."

Eleonore smiled wanly.

"I daresay," the woman chatted, "I wonder why Lady Leighton has not mentioned that you are here. I met her yesterday at a bridge party, you know."

Eleonore felt the blood leave her face. "I have to go now—" she began.

"Yes, yes, you must be very busy. Don't let me keep

you. I will send you Betty's sister, gladly. She can also cook."

In the end, she could get rid of Mrs Glissing only after she'd accepted the help. Maybe it was not such a bad idea to clean the house and make sure everything was in order. And it would help to have someone around who could cook.

"But only for a fortnight," Eleonore impressed on her.

"Yes, yes." Mrs Glissing went down the front steps with a smile, then turned. "I am *so* glad you have returned. It was about time. Oh, and Violetta." She went up the stairs again. "It would please us very well, Mr Glissing and myself, if you were to join us at the Blackwater ball Saturday next. Lady Blackwater will be thrilled to extend the invitation to you once she learns you are in town. She and Madelyn have been such close friends."

"Thank you, but I do not think I will have time, Mrs Glissing."

"Oh, but then you should make some time. This is a very important opportunity that is not to be missed. I will send you an invitation. But first, I will send you Betty and Annie."

Betty arrived faster than expected, with a big basket. "Mrs Glissing sends it, ma'am." The basket was stuffed not only with food but also with a bottle of wine. Eleonore took the basket, touched. Even though Mrs Glissing was a gossip, she had a good heart.

"And this is my sister, Annie. She can cook, clean, and sew."

"I can also hack wood." Annie flexed her arm. "As good as any man."

"I am impressed." Annie seemed to be capable, indeed.

After her curtsy, she immediately disappeared to sweep the floor.

"Mrs Glissing sends this as well." Betty handed her a card. It was the invitation to the ball. Eleonore looked at it with furrowed eyebrows. She knew better than anyone that one best met the high and mighty on their turf: at soirees, dinner parties and balls. Since she was alone in town, she couldn't attend balls on her own. But with the company of the Glissings, it would be a different matter altogether. Attending the ball would allow her to not only meet her patrons but also meet new ones. It was an opportunity not to be missed.

She would have to buy herself a new ball gown, shoes, and a shawl. The dress she was wearing now was given to her by Mrs Benningfield, bless her, otherwise, she would still run around in her nightgown, since her entire wardrobe had burned to cinders. But the plain, brown cotton dress was not something she could wear in society.

She would have to go shopping.

But first, she had to do something even more important.

CHAPTER SIXTEEN

Parliamentary Intelligence

The Duke of ROCHFORD proposed a Motion on the reform of education specifically regarding women, and the establishment of a national system of education in general, to be brought under the consideration of the house.
Lord HALSFORD seconded the Motion with enthusiasm, stating that the current system of
Education, specifically regarding women, is defective and in dire need of reform.
Lord TYBALT strongly objects to the Motion on the argument that there is no necessity for reforming something that seems to be working well and that it is neither practicable nor advantageous for women to receive any institutionalised education, and that doing so would do more harm than good.

*H*e couldn't stop thinking about her.

It was most infuriating.

He'd fled Bath to rid himself of the meddling, quarrelsome, prim woman, only to find he couldn't eradicate her from his mind.

It occurred to him he hadn't looked at Adika's painting since the night of the fire, and he also hadn't had those nightmares anymore. They had stopped the moment he'd told Eleonore about them. His hand searched his pocket. The trinket wasn't there. Maybe he'd left it on his nightstand?

He'd been entirely wrong about Eleonore. For her meddling turned out to be concern for her students; her quarrelsomeness was honest outspokenness, a trait he admired in men because of its rareness, and she wasn't at all as prim as she led him to believe. There was sizzling passion bundled up behind the stiff exterior that she showed the world. She was curvy, soft, and malleable underneath, and he had figured out quickly how to get that iron rod in her spine to melt. It had been surprisingly easy.

And those lips!

He was aware that he was daydreaming again. He shifted in his seat and tugged at his cravat. Back in his usual club in London, he sat in a leather armchair perusing a newspaper, except he found his attention was with her instead of on the news of the day. It was profoundly perturbing and most inconvenient.

He'd found a small article that declared "Renowned Girls School burned to cinders in Bath, everyone dead," followed by another article in another newspaper that declared "Duke of Rochford a national hero." He'd saved not only the school but the entire street and St James's palace from burning down. Never mind that the school was in Bath and the palace in London. Both his cheeks had burned with embarrassment as he skimmed the article.

How it came that no one had died would perpetually remain a mystery to him. They insisted on calling him a hero merely because he hauled out several of those scruff-necked children, which anyone in his right mind would have done. The look of hero-worship in their eyes had unsettled him. Then he'd seen a disturbingly similar look in *her* eyes, and he realised it was time to do what he always did when he found himself on the verge of getting emotionally involved: run.

The farther the better.

He tapped his finger impatiently on the newspaper. India was a splendid notion. He'd not only rid himself of this terrible English weather but also of the meddling woman with the silver eyes. He could see what his former ward and her blasted viscount were up to. It was a good plan.

Except the ship wasn't leaving until next month, and he had no clue what to do in the meantime. This was a problem he wasn't normally accustomed to. The notorious Duke of Rochford normally slept until the early afternoon, ate, went to the club, and afterwards whiled away his days and nights in the gaming hells and bordellos of London. But thanks to the dratted rooster (he had been chagrined to learn that creature had survived the fire), his body had accustomed itself to awakening regularly at pre-dawn. He was most disgruntled that his body kept up the same rhythm in London. He'd stare at the canopy of his four-postered bed, unable to fall asleep, wondering whether he should start the day at five in the morning.

He'd tried a gaming club afterwards, but it had seemed oddly insipid. The problems his cronies moaned about seemed paltry, for who cared whether they lost their fortunes? Others nearly lost their lives in a terrible fire, and did they complain? No. They pulled up their sleeves and organised their students into little groups, wrote letters to their parents and made sure they were all well taken care of.

He'd been irritated with his playing partners and lost heavily. Then he tried his favourite bordello only to find the women there too perfumed, too gaudily dressed, and too artificial in word, demeanour, and dress. When Peggy sat on his lap and grinned at him, exposing a set of yellow-black teeth, and he inhaled a whiff of sweat inter-mingled with rancid perfume and alcohol, he felt physi-cally unwell. He pushed her from his lap and left without a word. He'd run about London on foot, disgusted with himself and the world.

He remembered Eleonore's smell of cleanness and lavender, her simple gowns, her fine silvery hair, and her clear skin and sparkling eyes. It was her fault that he'd lost his taste for the doxies. 'Pox on her!

Utterly desperate, he did something which he never did. He got up in the middle of the night and wrote a speech, which he presented to the House of Lords. He hardly ever set foot in the place, but for once he felt inspired to stand up and see whether something could be done to improve the education of women. Miss Hilversham would have approved. Not that her approval mattered to him. Well, maybe a little. He'd done it mainly because it amused him to stir up a beehive. For, of course, he'd come up with fierce resistance. Only Halsford supported his motion because his wife used to be a teacher at Miss Hilversham's seminary. The rest of the lot, cowards and blighted idiots all, saw no reason to educate women, because, no doubt, they were terrified of a woman who was capable of thinking. It would take a long time before such a reform could finally be implemented. Until then, schools like Miss Hilversham's needed all the help they could get.

He growled.

"Why, Rochford! You haven't graced this club with your presence in quite a while. Are we to be honoured to find you here?" The annoyingly nasal voice belonged to Lord Stanhope, who considered himself to be a Nonpareil, but, with his pink waistcoats and polka-dotted coats, came across as a clownish dandy.

"Stanhope." Rochford lifted one corner of his mouth.

The man sat across from him without waiting to be invited. "London is so dull at this time of the year, with the season not yet starting and everyone out and about in the country—but what do my eyes behold?" He waved his manicured hand at Rochford.

"What?"

Stanhope pulled out his quizzing glass, bent forward and stared. "What on earth are you drinking, my good man?"

"Oh. This?" Rochford lifted his glass. "I believe they call it milk."

Stanhope's mouth dropped a few inches.

"You may close your mouth," Rochford said, bored.

He snapped it shut. "So, this is what happens?"

"Do stop speaking in riddles. What the blazes do you mean?"

"One rusticates in the countryside for several weeks and returns with a propensity for wearing—" he gestured at Rochford's cravat, which was crumpled and half-opened as he'd kept tugging at it constantly, "this, and drinking—that?"

"I was in Bath. Not sure that qualifies as countryside, but I suppose it's close."

"Bath!" Stanhope swallowed. "I am to spend the next week with my fiancée in Bath, drinking the waters. The thought of me leaving the place with an affinity for m-m-milk is rather disturbing."

"You should try it, old man." Rochford lifted his glass and swirled it around. "It's ambrosia for the soul." He leaned forward and whispered. "This has to stay between us. This is the secret of my conquests. It is my secret aphrodisiac."

Stanhope's eyes widened. "You don't say!" He snapped his fingers and called the butler. "Bring me some of what he's drinking. Immediately."

The butler brought a glass of cold milk, and Stanhope took it gingerly and looked at it as if it could bite. Then he took a sip, pulled a face, and took another.

"Can you feel it already?" Rochford struggled to keep his face deadpan.

Stanhope closed his eyes. Then grinned. "I believe I do!"

"Well, then. Excellent." Rochford was laughing inwardly but did not move a muscle in his face. "Now, you must drink it in silence, otherwise your bodily system won't absorb its aphrodisiac qualities. You understand?"

"Oh yes. Silence. Absolutely!"

So, it came that both men were sitting in silence sipping their milk.

The other gentlemen in the club lowered their newspapers and stared.

"What the deuce are they doing?" whispered one. "Is this a hoax?"

"I believe they are drinking—milk?"

"But why?"

"Is it the new fashion?"

"But this is the Duke of Rochford! One barely knows his face anymore. This is the most hardened gambler, womaniser, and drinker London has ever produced. Did you hear he is a hero now? Did you hear his speech in the House? It has caused quite a stir. If this fellow has turned to drink milk, there must be a reason. Butler?"

"I have overheard His Grace to say it is for the er, aphrodisiac qualities in the drink," the butler said with a straight face.

"Bring me one immediately."

Thus, within a few moments, he'd managed to transform the hard drinkers of White's into imbibers of milk. When Rochford left the club a few hours later, he heard a panicking undertone in the butler's voice as he instructed the footman that he was to buy more milk from the market as they were running low. What fools!

That had been one of his most amusing incidents so far.

The rest was profound boredom.

There was nothing that London could offer him that would eliminate that boredom.

The only thing that interested him was in Bath.

Confound it!

Maybe he should return.

After all, he ought to enquire into how the renovations of the school were going, whether all the pupils had been picked up, especially Little May, and by Jove, what she'd done with the blasted rooster. It nearly hurt him physically to admit that he even missed its crowing.

He'd attempted to sketch an outline of the new school. Merely to amuse himself. It ended up being a detailed architectural plan with four floors. The new school would be, in its foundations, twice the size of the original. The classrooms would be bigger, as well as the common area and the dining room. There would be a more spacious library and an office where she would work....He'd whiled away an entire afternoon with the design.

He wondered whether she'd met her patrons. The amount of work that needed to be done to convince the parents to send their children back was momentous. The school had suffered massive damage to its image, and one needed to do some, no, quite a bit of advertising. She ought to take advantage of the newspapers, not only the ones in Bath but the ones in London, *The Times*, for instance...had she thought of that? Also, he'd neglected to ask how she was planning on reaching the influential aristocrats. He supposed he could help. But with his reputation, that was doubtful. Would she welcome his help?

He barked a laugh.

Then he sighed.

How many days were left until the ship left for India?

It was mid-afternoon now, and he had no idea what to do. He put on his coat and took his carriage home. Maybe he could read a book. Apparently, he had a library. He wondered what kinds of books she liked to read.

His carriage turned a corner and stopped. He heard his coachman shout in anger; no doubt a pedestrian nearly ran into his horses, a common occurrence here in London —when he glanced outside the window.

Dash it all, now his mind was playing tricks on him. This was what happened when one constantly thought about a person: you saw them in earnest. For that figure, tall, lithe, in a dark blue coat, scurrying down the street— it looked like her. But Eleonore never scurried, so it couldn't be her, especially not in that stooping manner. But that light silver hair under the bonnet? Only one person had that kind of hair.

"Stop the carriage!" Marcus roared, tore the door open and jumped out before the carriage came to a halt.

It couldn't be her. She scuttled back and forth, took a few steps, and retraced them, muttering to herself like a half-wit.

"Miss Hilversham? Eleonore?" He grabbed her by the arm and whirled her around. The woman looked up, and her gaze hit him in the heart. Her eyes were swimming in tears. "What is the matter? Are you hurt?" By Jove, if someone had assaulted her...

She focused on him. "You! Why are you here?" She sniffled and wiped her eyes. Her spectacles were gone.

"What has happened?"

He saw emotions battle on her face. Resentment. Relief. Resignation. "I need to go in there."

"Where?" They were in the middle of a forsaken street

somewhere in London. It was half drizzling and cold and grey—his eyes fell on the massive iron gate in front of him.

Everything in him stilled as he recognised the building. They were standing in front of the Foundling Hospital.

The woman slumped against him. "I need to get them to tell me where she is. I know what they will say. The answer is no. Always no. But I need to ask, anyway. It is the fifteenth of August, you see. I must at least ask." She sniffed.

It was strange how, despite that incoherent speech, all the puzzle pieces suddenly came together.

"Yours?" His voice sounded hoarse.

He thought she would never reply.

She gave an infinitesimal nod.

Good heavens.

CHAPTER SEVENTEEN

The Governors of the Foundling Hospital
hereby give notice that the Hospital will reopen for Admission
on August 15th. Woodrow, Secretary

"Absolutely not!" He backed away.

"Please." She, proud Miss Hilversham, head-mistress of a school, who never begged, looked like she was about to go down on her knees in the middle of the wet street to plead for his help. "I have no one else to ask." Her eyes glittered with unshed tears, and there was a line of pain around her mouth that he'd not seen before.

The woman wanted him to accompany her inside the Foundling Hospital, which was an orphanage—for illegitimate children. No man in his right mind would put a foot in the place.

He rubbed his temple. "Confound it, woman. You're trembling. Oh, very well. Here, hold on to my arm, lest you end up collapsing in the middle of the street and then I'll have to carry you."

He was certain that he must have lost his mental faculties when he agreed to step with her through the forbidding iron gates. There were three imposing buildings arranged in a U-shape around a courtyard. As they walked along the side of the courtyard towards the left building, she seemed to calm down somewhat.

"Where to now?" He shot her a sideways glance. She walked with her head hanging down and would've run into a lamp post if he hadn't guided her around it at the last minute.

On the right side of the yard, a large group of women lined up to enter one of the building's doors. Each carried a bundle or held a small child.

Eleonore began trembling again. "I can't do this," she whispered.

Marcus crushed her hand in his grip. "We came all the way here, and even though I do not know what we are about to do, we're going to do it. Do we stand in line with these women?"

She shook her head. "To the secretary's office. On the left."

The porter admitted them, and before Marcus could enquire what they should do next, they were ushered into a cramped office. A man stood up from a desk. "How may I help you?"

It was her turn to state her business, but instead of speaking, she hung her head again. Since the man kept his gaze on him, he supposed he ought to say something.

Marcus cleared his throat. "It appears we are looking for um, err, ah," he threw her an exasperated look and resisted the impulse to elbow her in the ribs, but she looked so wretched that he took pity on her.

"A child, maybe?" the man put in helpfully.

"Ah yes. A child, I suppose."

"I understand." The man evidently understood more than Marcus did. "The certificate, please?"

"The what?"

"I am happy to be of help if you could give me the certificate." The man raised an eyebrow.

Eleonore slumped. "I don't have any certificate."

"Madam. I am unable to find the child in the registry without the certificate. It must have been given to you at the reception of the child."

"Can you please just look her up in the registry? 1804, August 15. Hope Hilversham." Her low voice shook.

The secretary took off his glasses with a sigh. "But that was nearly eighteen years ago! It is virtually impossible to find the child—who is now an adult—in the numerous tomes we have in the archives without a number. I am afraid I am unable to help."

Marcus supposed it was his turn to say something. "Listen, man. Surely you keep precise bookkeeping here, and it can't be so difficult to pick out the books of the year and look up which children were admitted on August 15, 1804? How many children could have been dropped off on that day?"

The man threw him a flustered look. "Hundreds."

"You're roasting me."

"If it was admission day, alas, I am not. Even if that were so, without any certificate as proof that you are the physical mother of the child, nor without the child's number, I am not at liberty to disclose this information to you or anyone else, for that matter."

Eleonore clasped her fingers so hard around Marcus' arm that her knuckles turned white. He'd probably end up having a bruise there.

"Well, I insist you do so anyhow." He bared his teeth.

The man threw him a mistrustful look. "Forgive me, sir. And you are?"

"Rochford."

The man smashed his glasses back on his thin nose. "Rochford?"

"Yes."

"The Duke of Rochford?"

"How many Rochfords are there in London? Of course, the duke."

"Your Gr-Gr-Grace!" The man bowed awkwardly. "I did not know."

Marcus decided he was an idiot.

"Forgive me for asking. But circumstances being as they are—considering Your Grace's presence here in person—might one assume—the question being—If it isn't too forward to ask—" he pulled out a handkerchief and wiped his forehead. "I humbly beg your pardon. But what exactly is your role regarding this child?" he blurted out.

Marcus thought swiftly. She was melting with grief right in front of his eyes, and all that stood between her and the information she wanted was that spindly idiot of a clerk. He had no patience with that sort of breed whatsoever. So, if he had to pull out his rank and power to accomplish something so they could finally leave this wretched place, he would do so. He might even go a step further. Reputation be damned.

"I'm the father, of course. Why else would I be here?"

He knew he'd sold his soul the moment he uttered those words, but damnation, he couldn't bear this any longer.

She was looking at him as though he had grown horns on his head. He leaned forward, restrained himself from grabbing the man at the collar, and said in a subtly threatening voice, "I suggest you go through those books and see what you can find. For if you are successful, I might be philanthropically inclined to leave a donation."

The man adjusted his collar. "O-Of course, Your Grace. In this case, it is an entirely different situation. I will attempt to find the information you seek. Could you write the information here, on this slip of paper?" He passed him a piece of paper and a pencil. Marcus passed it onto Eleonore, who swiftly scribbled the date and the name on the paper.

Marcus took the pencil, thought for a moment, then jotted down a figure on top of the paper and circled it. "Do you see this figure?"

"Yes, Your Grace," the man said with wide eyes.

"This is the figure I intend to donate, but only if you are successful."

"Your Grace!"

"And it is to be monthly."

After the clerk recovered from his astonishment, he became quite officious. "I will find the information, Your Grace. It will take some time, Your Grace. Might I suggest His Grace tours the hospital in the meantime? It might require several hours at the least."

Several hours? That did not appeal to His Grace at all. "Isn't there a coffee room somewhere?" he grumbled.

"Indeed, Your Grace, Guildford Street has a charming tearoom that I would recommend."

"Tea room it is. You have two hours. We shall return," Marcus pulled out his pocket watch, "at five o'clock sharp."

"Thank you," she whispered, so quietly he thought he'd imagined it.

Mrs Edgar's Tea Room was every bit as grungy inside as it looked on the outside. The furniture was threadbare, the chairs rickety, and the fat woman who greeted them wiped her hands on a greasy apron and looked at them curiously through little beady eyes. She recognised nobility immediately, for it wasn't every day The Quality graced her humble tearoom.

They took a table by the window and ordered tea and seed cake. The past half an hour had put Eleonore through the wringer. After they'd entered the office, she'd nearly collapsed with relief when she saw that there was a new secretary. It was no longer the nasty Mr Wimple, who'd been most unhelpful in the past, but a younger man, who, to her disappointment, seemed to be equally unhelpful. If it hadn't been for the duke, she would have had to leave once again without the information she sought. Like so many other times before. Seventeen times, to be exact.

"Well, Miss Hilversham." Rochford leaned back and looked at her through heavy lids. "I am waiting."

"I suppose I owe you an explanation." Eleonore took a piece of cake and crumbled it on her plate.

He drummed his fingers on the table.

But where to begin? It wasn't an easy story to tell. She hadn't told it to anyone, not even to her beloved godmother, Madelyn, not in its entirety. How odd that she found herself sitting in this seedy tearoom, telling her story, baring her soul to none other than the Duke of Rochford.

He had a right to know.

"I was barely fifteen when I ran away from my family's estate," she began. "My father had insisted to betroth me to a virtual stranger, and I would have none of it."

"Of course not." He took a sip of tea and grimaced. "Terrible brew." He heaped in three spoonfuls of sugar. "But continue. So, you ran away. Somehow, I would not have expected anything less of you. You must have been as headstrong as a child as you are now. I wager even more so."

Eleonore glared at him again. "So you are that kind of listener, the kind who has to provide unnecessary commentary after every sentence. If you would stop interrupting, I would be most grateful."

He folded his arms and smirked. "Not happening. I am far too intrigued. This is better than a scandal sheet. It begs commentary. Pray continue."

"My godmother took me in. I daresay she may have been glad to have a companion."

"Name?"

She sighed. "Does it matter? Oh, very well. Lady Madelyn Adkins."

He whistled. "The socialite? Even I have heard of her,

and I don't frequent those elevated circles. Far too intellectual for my taste."

"Yes, the socialite. I daresay I was a bit of an experiment for her as well, as she enjoyed giving me an education. Her kind of education, of course. I was allowed to partake in her social circles and meet all sorts of interesting people."

"Such as?"

"Wordsworth. Byron. Coleridge."

"She turned you into a bluestocking. That explains it, of course."

"Explains what?"

"Your penchant for being so—superior. Intellectually superior, I mean."

That took her aback. "I am?"

He wagged his curly black head back and forth. "Now and then. It is a characteristic that is most off-putting at first, but the longer I know you, I have come to think— but that is neither here nor there. Continue."

She wondered what he was going to say.

"So, I did not receive the conventional coming out that a girl my age would have had. My father washed his hands of me and seemed happy I was at least in London, acquiring some town bronze."

"And your mother?"

She shrugged. "Mother did whatever father wanted."

"Any siblings?"

A feeling of wistfulness overcame her. "One brother."

"Go on."

Pinching her lips together, she swallowed. Then she continued. "It was at one of those events that I met him. He was one of Byron's cronies. They were artistic, wild, beautiful and entirely unconventional, and for an impressionable sixteen-year-old, far too fascinating." She stared sightlessly at her plate, which was full of yellow cake crumbles.

"Sixteen! By George. That's precocious, to say the least. Let me guess how it continues. 'He' as you so mysteriously call him, did what my kind does all too well, and inevitably you found yourself with child."

She folded the napkin into tiny triangles. "It was very simple. I fell in love."

He snorted. "You should have known better. As should he."

"Says London's notorious rake. How many innocents have you seduced, I wonder?"

"My dear, I have, in my long and debauched life, bedded all sorts of creatures but certainly never ruined an innocent. Wouldn't touch them with a mile-long pole. One must stay away from them at all costs, lest one find oneself married. Rule number one for a rake." He helped himself to a piece of cake.

"Well, he certainly didn't marry me." She lifted her chin. "Are you shocked now that the prim Miss Hilversham has a scarlet past?"

"Nothing ever shocks me." He bit into his cake and grimaced. "I take that back. This cake shocks me. It is drier than Sahara dust."

She looked at him pensively. "I wonder…if it is not too forward to ask. But no, forget it. Let me continue."

"Ask. I am intrigued."

"How many do you have?"

"How many what?"

"Illegitimate children."

He choked on his cake. "By Jove!" He uttered in between coughs. "What a thought! Certainly not!"

"You mean you don't have them at the Foundling Hospital, or you don't have any illegitimate children at all?"

"I don't have any brats. Not as far as I know."

"But you can't know that, can you?" She leaned forward, chin in her hand.

"I'm a duke. If that were the case, you can count on them knocking at my door for funds and my name, begging me to acknowledge the brats. Not that I ever would. It is a moot point since it hasn't happened. Thank the heavens. Why are you looking at me in this odd way?"

"You are a strange man." A little smile flitted over her face. "You say you wouldn't acknowledge your own illegitimate child, a behaviour which I consider utterly reprehensible and thoroughly disgraceful, by the way. Yet only moments ago, you publicly acknowledged a child whose father you are certainly not. That is remarkably contradictory, wouldn't you say?"

He looked thoroughly put out. "It is an entirely different matter altogether. We would still be arguing with the secretary if I hadn't done so. But we stray off-topic, and you were about to tell me what happened after you discovered you were with child."

"I was sent to the country." It had been a disaster, but she'd been content staying with the farmer and his wife as she waited for Hope's birth. She'd had every intention of keeping and raising her child. She pulled out the trinket with the hair and stared at it. "Hope already had hair when she was born. And big, wise eyes. I was determined to make it work, you know." Her eyes were haunted by the memory.

"And the father?"

Her face hardened. "Denied from the very first that she was his. He wanted nothing to do with us, and a few months later, he left to fight in the war on the continent. He never returned."

"Your parents?"

She looked down at her lap. "We'd already become estranged long before that. I came down with childbed fever. It was a miracle that I did not die." They had talked to her while she was in a fever, delirious, hardly knowing what was real and what was a dream. She twisted the napkin on her lap. "After I recovered, the child was gone, and no one could or would tell me where she was."

She'd broken down. Her godmother had taken her in again, but Eleonore had withered away and lived like a ghost in her house. When Madelyn lay dying, she told her she would inherit her entire fortune. "Take it and go away. Travel, or what is better yet, reinvest it in something. Do something with your life, child. You are still young."

"It hardly matters what happens to my life now, Madelyn," Eleonore had replied.

Madelyn had gestured to an envelope on her nightstand. "It is for you. I dared not give it to you out of fear that it would make you regress again. But I see now that you need it. Take it."

She'd opened the envelope and poured its content onto her palm. It was a few strands of her child's hair.

She stared at it in disbelief. Then she understood. "It was you. You took my child away from me." The godmother she'd so admired, whom she thought she loved and was loved by, had betrayed her.

Madelyn sighed. "You were in no condition to take care of the child. She is better off where she is now. My advice would be to let it go and to rebuild your own life with the fortune you are about to receive."

Eleonore had jumped up. "Or I can find my child and build a future for us together," she'd said with burning eyes.

"Violetta. Be reasonable." The aunt leaned back into her pillows and closed her eyes. "A single unmarried woman with a child has no future. You know that as well as I do."

"I will never forgive you for this."

"It was what was best for you. Maybe I was wrong. Do what you must do." Those had been her godmother's last words.

Eleonore had immediately gone to the hospital to reclaim Hope.

But she received the answer that without a certificate or proof that she was the mother, they could not help her. Her aunt had hired an outsider to take the child, so she did not know the identity of the woman. Eleonore had scoured the entire house for the certificate, but there was none.

Every year, on August 15, she went to the hospital, and every year she'd received the same answer.

With the money her godmother left her, she founded the school in Bath.

After she'd told her story, she fell quiet.

Rochford's chin sank to his chest, and he brooded over her words. "So, since you couldn't raise your own child, you raised everyone else's. It makes very much sense."

"It is a sad story, is it not? I suppose I can count myself lucky that I did not end up in the gutters like so many other women. Thanks to Madelyn's money," she pulled a face, "which I decided to take even after she'd betrayed me."

"I cannot imagine any fate in which you would end up helpless in the gutters. You're too resourceful and pigheaded for that." He looked at his pocket watch. "Time is almost up. We have to return. Do you think that secretary will have the answer you seek?"

"I doubt it, but at least I have tried."

Back at the hospital, the secretary welcomed them with a mournful face. "There is no Hope Hilversham recorded in the books. I searched everywhere." He was disconsolate.

"Let me see the register." Marcus reached out for the thick leather tome.

In neat handwriting, column after column, child after child was registered, with a number, and a description of the token that was left.

"What is the meaning of token?" Marcus pointed at the word.

"A token is something the mother would have left with the child as a remembrance, or as yet another identifying factor. What token have you left?"

"I don't know. Someone else left the child in my stead."

"Well, that would explain why your name is not showing up in these books. It could be anyone then."

The man had not lied. There were nearly a hundred children registered for the day.

"Make us a copy of this page," Marcus ordered.

"I have already done so." The secretary handed her the paper.

She clutched the page. Her eyes flew over the list of names, none familiar. Without a specific name, it was like searching for a pearl at the bottom of the river Thames.

They climbed into the duke's carriage, and a heaviness fell over her limbs. Her head pounded, and the trembling started again. She rubbed her arms.

"Where to?" the duke asked. She gave him her address.

They rode silently to her townhouse.

She leaned her head back. Exhaustion swept over her so that she could barely hold herself up. The carriage stopped. He helped her out.

"You can barely walk," she heard him say through a pillow of cotton.

He supported her up the front steps. She dropped the key three times until he took it out of her hands and opened the door for her.

The empty, dark foyer gawked at her, now cleaner than before, and the smell of lemon and floor wax lingered in the air. Annie had gone somewhere, and she would be all alone with her memories in the big, empty house.

"Please," she turned to clutch his lapels, "Please stay."

"Dash it, Eleonore, you're not going to—" she heard him say from far, far away, but she no longer took in what, for darkness took hold of her.

CHAPTER EIGHTEEN

The Duke of Rochford,
*in the company of an unknown lady, has been seen visiting The
Foundling Hospital for charitable purposes. The Secretary, Mr
Woodrow, has confirmed that a sizeable donation has been most
humbly and gratefully received.*

Someone carried her up the stairs, mumbling and grumbling.

Someone pulled off her wet boots and loosened her corset. She sighed in relief.

Someone wrapped her in a blanket. "You're ill, Eleonore. You're completely burning. Is there anyone I should call aside from the leech?"

She felt a warm hand tuck away the strands of hair from her face.

"Ned," she mumbled. "Ned."

"Who the devil is Ned?" he demanded testily.

Ned was running over the meadow, flying a kite. Ned, with his shoulder-long hair and his cheerful smile. Ned, who followed her everywhere she went. She tried to explain it to him but found herself sucked into a fever dream.

Her daughter was dancing in the meadow with flowers in her long hair.

"You have grown so fast," Eleonore told her and took her hand.

"I have looked for you everywhere, Mama," Hope told her. And in the depths of her eyes, she could see the reflection of herself. Then a big gust of wind came and blew her away, like a leaf in the wind.

She tried to hold on to her hand, but the wind was too strong. She cried in anguish.

"Shh, shh, it's just a dream," another voice said, a calming voice, a soothing voice. She felt something cold on her forehead. Something warm and sweet in her throat, she spluttered.

"Stop spitting out the elderflower tea. Can you stop being so stubborn, for once? Swallow. Please? Swallow?"

Then she got sucked up into deeper, darker dreams without Hope and Ned.

There was a voice far, far away, begging her to get well again. Begging her not to die. She considered it for a moment. But it is so much nicer to die, she wanted to say. No more pain, no more suffering.

But the pleading voice wouldn't let her go. In a moment of clarity, she opened her eyes and discovered she was lying in a room with a light blue canopy above. She did not know where she was.

Voices were talking in the room, male voices.

"I cannot guarantee it, Your Grace. The fever is very strong. It is burning her up. If it doesn't break by nightfall…"

"I beseech you, doctor…."

Doctor? Why was there a doctor? She needed no doctor. She just needed to sleep.

"Please don't die," he begged again.

She'd heard that voice before, and sensed his presence next to her in some moments.

She forced her eyes open; the lids were heavier than lead.

"Marcus," she whispered. He lifted her hands and brought them to his cheek. It was rough with unshaved stubble and wet.

"Why are you crying?" She was feeling rather well now. Like floating on clouds. She remembered something. Something important which she wanted to tell him. "You and Hope," she formed with her dry lips, "You and Hope."

"What about me and Hope?" She heard the exasperation in his voice.

"I love the most."

She felt oddly light and at peace after that.

"Oh, no you don't. You hate me, remember?" he said roughly. "We fight all the time."

She wanted to deny it. She wanted to tell him he was the best, kindest man she'd ever met, that he had a heart that was too big for this world, and everyone misunderstood him, that was all. She wanted to tell him that, but she was tired, so tired.

"You have to get well again quickly, so you can keep on hating me." There was a strain of panic in his voice. "I intend to turn your school into a gambling den…" And then he said something more, but a roaring filled her ears, and she felt pulled under, and she was so ready to let go.

Why? He asked himself over and over.

Yet again a woman in his arms, dying.

Yet again the utter helplessness that filled him, the bleak despair, the hopeless love.

Who had put this curse on him?

After she'd said those words, her eyes huge and luminous, already more in the other world than here, he knew he'd lost. He never even had a chance.

He looked down at her, her fine hair clinging to her wet forehead, her skin pasty and wet. She muttered in her fitful sleep, full of nightmares.

Marcus pulled a hand over his wet face, got up, and stepped up to the window. He stared out of the window into the grey, wet London sky. He clasped his other hand into a fist and smashed it into the wall. It left his knuckles red and bruised. Cursing, he shook his throbbing hand.

She was one of the strongest, most beautiful souls he'd ever had the honour of knowing.

When had he begun to love her? Was it that very first day when she marched down the driveway toward him, scolding him like a sparrow whose nest was about to be disturbed?

A ghost of a smile flitted over his lips as he remembered those days. Ah, how he'd enjoyed goading her. He enjoyed their fencing, how she parried when he lunged, and how she met each of his barbs with caustic wit and spirit.

An insistent knocking on the front door echoed through the house and startled him out of his thoughts.

Maybe it was Fariq? He'd sent for the man, in addition to his butler, a footman, a cook, and an additional maid or two. A footman tapped lightly on the door.

"A visitor, Your Grace."

"I'm not in."

The footman shuffled. "Yes, Your Grace. However, it appears these visitors won't be swayed and insisted on waiting in the drawing room." He lifted a card, but Marcus waved it away impatiently.

As he stepped into the freshly dusted and polished drawing room, a couple rose from the sofa. He was a tall, slim, blonde-haired man, and the woman was elderly and a head shorter.

"Yes?" he barked. The faster he could get rid of them, the better, and to Jupiter with manners and etiquette.

The young man looked at him frostily. "Who are you?"

Marcus returned the antagonistic look with even greater frostiness. "My name is Rochford."

There was consternated silence.

The woman's hand crawled to her mouth. "Rochford?"

Ah. It seemed his reputation preceded him once more.

"Confound it. The wicked duke?" The man breathed. A light of fascination entered his eyes. "I've only read about you. You're legendary. Are you really him?"

"What can be the meaning of this?" The woman looked like she was about to burst into tears.

"I heard you have acquired hero status."

Marcus rolled his eyes and shrugged. "It's lies. All lies."

The man eyed him with open curiosity. "Did you really strip three gentlemen out of their fortunes in one entire night over a game of piquet?"

"Four." His face was deadpan.

"And is it true that you have a mistress lodged in each district in London?"

"Ned!"

"I beg your pardon, Mama."

"No, I do not have a mistress lodged in each district of London," Marcus replied testily.

The man's face fell.

"I have them lodged in each of the counties throughout the kingdom, of course. And," he added in an afterthought, "in the provinces of India, too. You do the math."

"Merciful heavens." The woman clasped her hands together.

"Having cleared up that highly important matter, let us move on to more relevant things. Your name is Ned?" Marcus folded his arms across his chest with a heavy frown. "Who the devil are you? What do you want, and why are you here?" If he was the former lover she'd mentioned in her fever dream, there was no doubt what he would do: he'd shoot a bullet through him on the spot.

The man pulled himself up. "I apologise. Did we not give a card to the footman? No matter. I am Leighton and this is my mother, Lady Leighton. We came here because Mrs Glissing, the neighbour, informed us that my sister, Miss Violetta Winford, has moved back into her old domicile. We wanted to call on her."

"You have been misinformed. There is no such person

here. This is the house of Miss Eleonore Hilversham, the headmistress of the selfsame seminary in Bath."

The woman sat and leaned her head back against the padding of the sofa as if it pained her. "Yes, yes. She calls herself that. Her real name is Violetta Winford. She is the daughter of the former Baron of Leighton, and my daughter."

He shot up an eyebrow. "You're Miss Hilversham's mother and brother?"

The two looked at each other and then back at him and nodded in unison.

Lady Leighton fiddled around with the pommels of her reticule. "Forgive me. I cannot help but wonder what *you* are doing in my daughter's house." The woman's glance travelled down his half-dressed appearance pointedly.

It hit him too late that he wasn't presentable and prob-ably looked like he just rose from his bed; his chin was stubbled, his hair dishevelled, and as usual, he'd forgotten to pull on his coat. His shirtsleeves were rolled up to the elbows, a corner hung out of his pants, and his pantaloons were rumpled.

No wonder their reception of him had been frosty. The mother and brother. This was a pickle, indeed.

How to get out of this?

He shrugged and said the first coherent thing that came to his mind. "Simple. We are married."

CHAPTER NINETEEN

DR RADCLIFFE'S PURGING ELIXIER
cleans the blood from all humours, impurities, and illnesses such
as fevers, colds, headaches, and gout. Available also in pill form
at your local apothecary.

*L*ady Leighton clapped her hand over her mouth, and the brother forgot to close his altogether.

"Violetta? A duchess?"

Marcus was done with the conversation. "I don't know any Violetta. But this is neither here nor there. Eleonore —is dying. So forgive me if I don't have time for this right now."

The mother paled.

"Good heavens. What happened?" Ned jumped up.

"A pernicious fever. The doctor was here, but he said he did all he could."

"I want to see her." Lady Leighton got up and pulled off her gloves. "Now."

Marcus supposed a mother had a right to see her dying daughter.

He led her up to the room.

AFTER SHE OPENED HER EYES, SHE SAW SUN RAYS GLIDE OVER the blue chequered bedcover.

For a moment, she was disoriented. This was not her bed in Bath.

Then it all came rushing back to her.

Her head felt raw, her tongue like a piece of leather. She turned her head. There was someone else in the room, a lady who was sitting on a chair next to the bed, her greyed head bent over embroidery. She wore purple mourning colours, and there was something familiar about her. The woman set her embroidery aside and placed a cool hand over her forehead.

"Violetta. My child."

"Mama," Eleonore whispered.

THEY SAY THERE IS SOMETHING ABOUT A MOTHER'S TOUCH that is healing. Maybe that was what brought Eleonore round, or maybe it was the tonics and teas that Marcus had instilled in her regularly and with such patience.

By evening, her fever had broken, and the worst was over. She felt weak, tired, and oddly light-headed, but she was fully awake.

When she awoke a second time, her eyes drifted to the person who sat in the armchair, deeply asleep.

His dark head rested against the back of the chair. There were dark rings under his eyes and his eyelashes curled against his pale cheeks.

"Marcus," she whispered.

His eyes popped open. He sat up. "You are awake."

"How long have I been ill?"

He pulled a hand through his tangled mane. "A week. Maybe longer. I lost count."

She gazed at him. "Were you here the entire time?"

"Your mother sat with you for a few hours, and I told her to retire while I took over the watch. She said you woke up earlier and recognised her and that the fever broke. I didn't believe it."

"Mother. Here. I thought I'd dreamed it."

"Your life was in great danger." His voice was rough. "Again."

"And you saved me," she said with a weak smile. "Again. It seems this is becoming a habit."

He brushed it away. "Nonsense. You were dangerously ill, and there was no one else to take care of you."

"I am sorry for all the trouble I put you through." She shook her head regretfully.

"You never chose to be ill, but you chose to walk into the burning school. There is a difference."

"I am feeling much better now. I wouldn't mind a bite to eat." Her pale hand attempted to push the bedclothes away, but he tucked them further up.

"Stay. I will fetch the maid. And your mother. Your brother is here, too, by the way."

"Ned?" She attempted to sit up. "He is here?"

"Ned." He rubbed his jaw. "You mentioned him in your

fever dreams. Might have told me he's your brother. Nearly wrung his neck when he showed up."

"Why?"

"Thought he was the man in your past."

A laugh escaped her lips. "Oh no. Ned and I were close when we were young. But I haven't seen him in a very long time."

He put his hand to the door latch and hesitated. "I will fetch your mother. I just want to say, there was a moment when you—" his throat moved as he swallowed, "—I was certain you were more in the other world than in this one. I am devilishly glad that you did not die." His voice was gruff.

"Marcus."

He turned. Their eyes met.

"Thank you," she whispered.

He nodded.

HER MOTHER ENTERED THE ROOM WITH A TRAY. SHE SAT BY Eleonore as she ate; the same quiet presence she remembered. They talked a little, then fell quiet. Her mother tucked the blanket in as if she were still a child and told her to go back to sleep.

Eleonore waited until she left the room.

She quietly slipped into a morning gown and walked down the stairs, holding on to the bannister. There were many people about, she noted. Was that a footman?

An unfamiliar maid rushed down the hallway, and the scent of cooking lingered in the air.

It was as if the house had come alive. Or as if her godmother had returned.

Standing at the entrance of the drawing room, she saw two men sitting at the table, playing cards.

The dark-haired one in shirtsleeves sprawled in his chair with an air of boredom and played out his cards as if he wasn't paying much attention to the game. Her eyes were glued on him, and she felt a fierce gladness rush through her.

Marcus.

The other gentleman she did not recognise at first. He was well dressed, of slighter build, with light blonde hair fashionably swept back. She gasped when she recognised him.

"Ned."

Both men whirled around to face her.

Marcus jumped up. "You should be in bed."

"Violetta." The man got up.

She moistened her lips. "You've grown up."

"So have you." He rubbed his neck.

She took a step towards him and felt her legs give way. Ned rushed forward and crushed her to him. "Now I am finally taller than you," he mumbled into her hair.

Eleonore sobbed into his coat.

"Should she be up? I don't think she should. This isn't good. Where's your mother?" Marcus sounded like a concerned hen.

"She is resting in her room. I am glad you are here." She held out her hand to him as she clung to her brother.

He took her hand and cleared his throat.

Ned beamed at her. "You could've told us, you know. Not only that you intended to come to town. But also, about your marriage. I would have liked to have been the best man."

"Marriage?" She blinked.

"Don't tell me the fever made you forget we married." Marcus's intent gaze pierced her.

"Oh." She stared at him wide-eyed. "I see. I almost forgot."

"It was a quick affair," Marcus tugged at his ear. "She fell ill immediately after. Everything was topsy-turvy. There was no time for anything, not even to send out an announcement."

"No, there was not," she said slowly.

"I only had time to do so this morning." Marcus hooked his thumbs in his pockets as he stood.

Her eyes widened in horror. He sent out their wedding announcement to the newspaper?

He made a silent motion with his hands as if to say, "What else was I supposed to do?" Her legs underneath her gave way, and she dropped onto a settee.

"Mrs Glissing," he mouthed quietly.

Her hand crawled to her mouth.

Good heavens.

Of course, that woman kept track of everyone who entered her house, and she would have seen him come and go. Marcus had to send off the announcement before she had the chance to trumpet to the world that the Duke of Rochford and Miss Hilversham had an improper liaison.

Eleonore swallowed.

Ned, not noticing anything off, said cheerfully, "I was certainly surprised to find you married. How on earth did you meet? You must tell me the entire story."

"There was a house in Bath," Eleonore began.

"There was a fire," Marcus said at the same time.

"It's a long story," Eleonore eventually said, and Marcus agreed by rolling his eyes.

"I have to tell you something, too." Ned took a turn about the room and stopped in front of her. "Father passed away recently. Did you know?"

"Mother told me." There was a lump in her throat. Her relationship with her father had never been good, and now he had passed on before she could do something about it.

"He was very ill and asked for you several times. We sent you a letter but never received an answer. Mother thought that you were not interested, so we left it at that."

Eleonore shook her head. "I never received those letters."

"Then Mrs Glissing came for a visit the other day and mentioned that you had moved back to town. So, we decided to visit. And we found him here." Ned nodded at Marcus. "Married to you."

She felt herself blush. She understood why Marcus had told this fib. It was in their best interest. How else to explain his presence here, especially if he never left her bedside while she was sick?

Her mother joined them and immediately fussed over her. "You ought to be in bed, child."

Marcus agreed, but since Eleonore refused, he forced her to sit on the sofa and wrapped her shoulders in a golden-orange Kashmiri shawl.

"How pretty it is." Eleonore's hand slid over the soft fabric. "Is it Indian?"

Marcus affirmed.

"We read about your school," her mother said while

the maid served tea. "What a disaster. I am profoundly grateful that nothing happened to you or your pupils."

"It is all thanks to the duke. He saved our lives, and he is a hero." She would blare it out from the tops of the roofs, so everyone knew.

He snorted, crossed his legs, opened a newspaper, and pretended the conversation did not pertain to him. But, in the meantime, she knew him better than that and saw the look of alert interest in his jade-green eyes.

"We read about the full extent of the disaster in *The Times*. We feared the worst."

Eleonore rubbed her eyebrow tiredly. "I had to send the students home, and His Grace was kind enough to allow some teachers to remain in his house, with a pupil or two who have no home to return to." She swallowed. "I intended to seek more financial support as the school now needs to be built from its foundations up."

Marcus lowered his paper and watched her with veiled eyes. "There is no need to tramp about town looking for patrons." He lifted a finger to call a butler, a man whom Eleonore had never seen before. She supposed he was one of Marcus's retainers.

The butler brought in a tray filled with letters.

"What is this?"

"Invitations from high and low."

She sifted through the letters. The duchesses of Threthewick and Dunross. Former pupils and teachers had written, expressing their horror at what happened, and offered help. There was even one from the Duchess of Ashmore, written from France, saying they would return immediately, to help her "dear friend and the best teacher I ever had."

"Frances, the Countess of Halsford, called while you were ill. I almost had to boot her out physically because she insisted on nursing you back to health single-handedly. I told her she'd be of more use if she could help raise some money for rebuilding the school. Looks like she took me at my word because the letters came flooding in soon after. And her husband's been debating in the House of Lords on the importance of female education and reform. A controversial topic, mind you. Many got up mid-debate and left."

"How would you know that?"

"I was there myself."

"You took up your seat in the House of Lords?" Eleonore could barely believe it.

"Shocking, isn't it? I presented a motion on the topic myself. But it isn't likely that this will come to pass soon. Nonetheless, Miss Hilversham's Seminary for Young Ladies was and still is well-beloved, more than one would think. Many remember you as Lady Adkins's ward, with much affection. Expect more invitations in the future."

Eleonore was overwhelmed by the sheer volume of solicitous messages of help and support.

She felt tears rise to her eyes. She felt oddly helpless. "Thank you." She gave him a quavering smile. "It seems lately all I am doing is thanking you."

Ned cleared his throat. "The thing is this: with all the high and mighty ones bowing down to you, sister, it would be good, after you have recovered, mind you, to show yourself more in society."

She nearly despaired at the sheer amount of work ahead of her and wanted to return to Bath as quickly as possible. But her brother was right. She had to answer those invitations….as the Duchess of Rochford? The thought alone gave her a headache. In what pickle did they get themselves into now? How on earth was she to navigate around this dilemma? Her eyes sought the duke's.

He averted his gaze. "I have some business to do. I believe Fariq is in town as well. He will report on what is happening at the school, currently." He left with a bow.

Eleonore knitted her brows and looked at her brother and mother, suddenly aware that she was alone with them for the first time in nearly two decades.

She knew nothing at all about her brother. And her mother … to her surprise, looked better than she ever did while her father was still alive. The mauve colour suited her, and even as she sat here embroidering and quietly listening to their conversation, she was not as self-effacing as she used to be.

"It was kind of you to come," Eleonore said formally, for one must say something.

"The Duke of Rochford." Ned made a silent whistle. "That's a big fish in the pond, sister. Who would've thought you had it in you?"

Her mother laid the embroidery aside. "He is a kind man. That is all that matters. I must admit, I was surprised, for one hears such unwholesome things… but then one ought not to listen to what one hears. I do not doubt that half of what is being said about people is either exaggerated or blatantly untrue. He proved all those gossipmongers wrong, for he saved you from that terrible fire. A person who does that can't be all that wicked. I am glad you married him, Violetta."

Eleonore shifted uncomfortably in her seat. Now was

probably not the time to tell them they were not married. That would lead to awkward questions that she wouldn't know how to answer. Eleonore felt her headache return. She would have to think about this later.

"We will have to have a ball. At Leighton House, of course." Leighton House was their London townhouse, which they had not used very often when her father was still alive, for he had always preferred the country. "But first, there is Lady Blackwater's ball. Mrs Glissing said you have received an invitation as well. Let us go together." Her mother took her hand. "Provided you feel better by then, of course."

A ball was the last thing Eleonore wanted. She intended to decline but felt as though all the fight had drained from her. It would make her mother happy. Her brother too. One ball, as the Duchess of Rochford. Afterwards, she could return to Bath. She and the duke could quietly go their separate ways, and everyone would return to their old lives.

As before.

She fiddled with the fringes of her shawl.

"My fiancée will be there too," Ned said cheerfully. "Lady Esther Mornay."

"Oh! I am so glad." Eleonore's face broke into a smile. "Are we to have a wedding soon?"

"In two months." Ned beamed. "You must meet her, Violetta. I think you will like her. But more of that later. I have an appointment at the club."

Ned took his leave. Eleonore saw his slim form retreat, feeling grateful that her brother was back in her life, and a little wistful that he was no longer the little imp she'd played with when she was younger.

Her mother's fingers fiddled with the pompoms on her reticule. "I don't know how to tell you how sorry I am for all the lost years. The estrangement between us. I regret many things that happened, that your father decided should happen, and I should have spoken up more. Defended you more. You were so young. I know I was wrong about keeping silent. Can you ever forgive me?"

Eleonore threw her a surprised look. She hadn't expected this from her mother. Could she forgive that they'd renounced her when she needed them the most? She found, upon reflection, that this was not what mattered to her anymore. The estrangement had been sustained from both sides.

"What about my baby?" she whispered. "I thought Madelyn had it arranged to take my baby away. It was you, wasn't it?"

Her mother's face froze. "It was both of us. Madelyn and I agreed it was best to have her taken to the Foundling Hospital. Try to understand, Violetta. Under the circumstances, it would've been impossible for you to keep the child. You were so young. And ill. And your father would have none of it."

"I was never consulted." Eleonore's eyes burned. "And they never let me say goodbye to the baby. One moment she was in my arms, the next she was gone. I don't know whether I can ever forgive that."

Her mother looked stricken. "I did not know that."

"Yet when I went to the hospital, they could find no records of the child. I thought it was sloppy bookkeeping. Or arbitrariness on behalf of the secretary. I went year after year, yet always received the same reply. I concluded that my child was never taken there."

Her mother shook her head. "It can't be. Molly herself took the child. She had strict instructions to take her to the hospital."

"Molly Barton?" Molly Barton had been serving at their parents' mansion since she could remember. She was a kind and honest woman and loyal to the Leightons.

"Yes. She assured me she left the child with a token. A lock of your hair, I believe. She also showed me the form for admission to the ballot. I saw it with my own eyes. You know they must draw a white ball for the child to get admitted."

Eleonore nodded. She knew that the women who petitioned for their child's admission had to draw a ball from a bag. A white one meant admission provided the child was healthy. An orange ball meant the child was temporarily refused but could take another's place if that baby failed the health check. A black ball meant refusal.

"Molly returned, saying she'd drawn the white ball. The child was admitted. There is no reason to doubt her."

"And yet," Eleonore's voice shook, "when I went there to claim my child, they told me there is not a single record of her. How do you explain that, mother?"

"I don't know why that would be, Eleonore." Her mother drooped her shoulders. "And we can no longer ask Molly. She left soon after."

"What makes you so certain she took the child there?" Eleonore insisted.

Her mother let out a weary sigh. "You are right. We cannot know for sure. We simply must believe that Molly did the right thing. I have no reason to doubt her."

"She may have taken the child and kept her for her own." Eleonore's voice shook. "You said she left soon after?"

Her mother shook her head. "No. Be reasonable. Why would a serving maid keep a child on her own? Molly had a difficult enough life as it was. The last thing she needed was to be a single mother with a child."

Her mother was right. Why would a serving maid want to burden herself with a child that was not her own? It was more likely that the child was admitted and adopted soon after, and for some reason or other, they lost the record.

Eleonore rose, clutching her shawl. "If you will excuse me, I need to lie down."

Back in her room, she retrieved with shaking fingers the register the secretary had copied. She scanned the rows of names.

But there was no Molly Barton on the list.

It had been so long ago.

It was difficult to reconstruct events that happened eighteen years ago. Maybe Molly had lied after all. Maybe she had given a different name. Maybe she'd told the truth, but the secretary had not done his job properly. Maybe he had and was then forced to take out all evidence of registration by the family who'd adopted the child. Maybe.

Eleonore stared at the lock of her child's hair, her thumb stroking the silken softness.

She was eighteen now. A young lady. Did she look like her? With white-blonde hair and grey eyes? Or more like Edward, with his thick, brown hair.

If she were honest with herself, she'd have to admit

that every time she'd admitted a pupil to her school, she'd searched her face for something, an inkling of something familiar, a trait, an expression, a movement that would indicate that she was her lost daughter. The habit had become so ingrained that she no longer noticed she did so.

Staring at the list of names, she tapped her finger against the paper. There was one more thing she could try. She sat down, pulled out a piece of paper and a quill, and wrote a short missive. She enclosed the sheet with the names.

"Deliver this to Mr Fariq at the Perpignol immediately. Tell him I await his reply," she directed the footman.

CHAPTER TWENTY

The grandest ball of this season
*Lady Blackwater's ball will be on Saturday, Nov 3. Everyone
with rank and name is expected to attend.
Dancing will begin at eight o'clock.*

*T*he ball was inconvenient and infuriating, and a nuisance through and through. Eleonore did not look any happier about it than he felt, even though she looked breathtaking in a night-blue dress trimmed with delicate Mechlin lace. Regal, proud. Not at all the prim schoolmistress he'd thought she was. She had recovered quickly from her illness, and even though her nose was pale, she looked, for all that it was worth, like a diamond of the first water. He'd stood for several moments searching for words, only to utter gruffly, "You'll do," when she first descended the stairs.

"So will you," she'd replied, dryly.

He supposed he cleaned up nicely when he wanted to. He'd shaved and put on his usual evening gear. Judging from her soft grey eyes, she liked what she saw. That was good.

He eyed the ballroom wearily. It was a bloody crush. He only had himself to blame since he'd got them into this muddle to begin with. What devil rode him to blurt out that they were married? He, the Duke of Rochford, marrying a schoolmistress. The thought alone was endlessly amusing, but deep down, he felt that there was nothing funny about it at all. When people came up to pump his hand and congratulate him, they seemed sincere, and he'd felt this odd rush of pride. And for a moment, it felt real.

Plague take it. They were riding deeper and deeper into this deception with every day that passed. How on earth were they ever to get out of this?

Yet he could hardly desert Eleonore when her family took her to a ball. It wouldn't look good if the husband were not there. So, he'd reasoned, he could show up, shock society with his reformed manners, throw some more food for gossip their way, and dance a dance or two with his *wife*. Not that this was a necessity, since husbands were not expected to dance attendance to their wives.

He knit his brows together as he saw her give her hand to a gentleman in burgundy. She seemed to have dancing partners aplenty. Far too many men flocked to her. He found he did not like that one bit.

After the dance, her partner led her from the ballroom floor to the chairs by the wall. There was a strain around her eyes. She shouldn't be dancing so much. She had only recently recovered from her deathbed, after all.

Marcus became more and more convinced that this entire ball was a bad idea, and it did not help in the least that he was responsible for it.

Scowling, he made his way across the ballroom floor. People melted out of his way.

There was another popinjay in front of him, bowing over her hand. She made a motion to stand up.

"Mine, I believe," Marcus intervened, completely disregarding the man.

"I beg your pardon, but Her Grace has just given me the honour of the next dance."

Marcus brushed him aside and took Eleonore's hand.

The man spluttered, but Marcus led Eleonore to the dance floor.

"You are behaving execrably," she hissed.

He felt something spark in him. It was happiness. Yes, definitely happiness. She'd recovered her spunk and was sparring with him again. How he'd missed it!

"A man ought to be allowed to dance with his wife at least once," he drawled.

"Except we're not really married, are we?" Her eyes shot up to meet his.

"With a parsimonious schoolmistress like you? We would argue from dusk till dawn over correct pronunciation and mannerisms." He imagined starting the day with spats over the breakfast table. He would tease her, and she would lecture him on his abominable language and deportment. His heart warmed at the idea.

"I am not parsimonious," she protested as the strains of music started up.

A waltz.

He swept her into his arms, and pulled her up close, closer than was appropriate, but he never gave a tuppence about what was appropriate anyhow. At the moment, he merely enjoyed having her so close that he could smell the lavender in her hair and see the silver sparks in her eyes.

He looked down at her possessively. "Yes, you are. Parsimonious, meddling, and quarrelsome. Now be quiet and dance."

"And you are a domineering, overbearing, quick-tempered, ill-mannered boor." She followed him easily as he swept her into a full turn. "Smile," she hissed. "The entire ballroom is watching us."

So they were. Curious faces turned towards them, watching their dance that was clearly an argument.

He pulled his face into a grimace of a smile. "It is because you are so teasable. I find that infinitely more entertaining than talking about the weather. So, you consider me an ill-mannered boor?"

"Don't look so pleased. It's not meant to be a compliment. But at least you know how to dance." Her grey eyes softened.

Yes, he knew how to waltz. It was his favourite dance. She was as light as a feather in his arms and followed his lead easily.

"Violetta." He tried the name on his lips. "What kind of a damnably frilly name is that? Doesn't suit you at all."

"Unfortunately, we don't choose the names we're given."

"But you chose Eleonore."

She shook her head. "It is my middle name."

"Violetta Eleonore," he tried the names and shook his head. "All fluff, cream, and roses, when in reality you are thorns, starch and vinegar. And claws. Madame Puss suits you infinitely more than Hilversham. Where did the name come from, anyway?"

"It's my godmother's surname. Madelyn Hilversham, Lady Adkins. But you are distracting from the problem at hand."

He raised an eyebrow. "And that being?"

"How we are going to untangle ourselves from this fiasco? I was initially thankful you came up with the idea, for this would have developed into a full-blown scandal otherwise. I dare not fathom the dimensions."

"Yes. Imagine the prim schoolmistress having an affair with the wicked duke. That wouldn't do at all," he mused. "Better have her married to him."

He watched, fascinated by how a delicious shade of puce crawled over her cheeks. And, for a change, she seemed entirely speechless.

"Except now, the longer we keep up the charade, the more difficult it will be to get out of it." He spoke the thoughts that seemed to worry her most, for a look of panic shadowed her face. "Never fear. When the time comes, I will think of something," he hastened to add.

Besides, he had plans to travel to India. He'd nearly forgotten all about that. When she'd nearly died, he'd fallen into this familiar black hole that skewed his ability to think properly. He'd expected to feel the pull again, to drown his sorrows in alcohol and opium. It hadn't happened. Come to think of it, ever since he'd met her, Marcus had not felt those cravings. Not even once. What a profound realisation to make on the ballroom floor in the middle of a waltz.

"The problem neither of us have considered when we precipitously and unthinkingly threw ourselves into this venture is that even if we separate amicably as some married couples do, it will not shed a good light on the school at all. Everything I—we—do now to revive the school will have been for nought."

She looked genuinely worried.

Thunder an' turf. He didn't want her to look worried. He wanted her to rant at him, scold him, and tell him he was an ill-mannered boor, even if they were in the middle of a waltz.

"Then let us do it," he said flippantly, turning her into another full turn. "Let's get the thing done and over with. We get married next week for real and make it official, and everyone will be happy. It is the perfect solution."

He felt her freeze in his arms, and she missed a step. "You must be joking?"

He held her up, and the dance continued. "In fact, I am not." He realised that his words, although spoken impetuously, were true.

"But I don't understand. How is this the perfect solution?"

"If I had my fingers available, I could use them to tick off all the reasons, but they are, alas, holding you so you don't sprawl all over the dance floor. So, tick them off mentally as I list them. Ready? One: you need not live in fear of anyone unmasking this sham marriage as it is real. Two: Your reputation is forevermore ensured; Miss Hilversham never had an inappropriate liaison with the wicked duke, and even if she did, it matters not since she has successfully hauled him into the matrimonial harbour. She has succeeded where hundreds of others have failed. Your elevation and admiration in the ranks of society are forevermore guaranteed."

"I don't care a tuppence for this," she snapped. "Besides, you rank your importance rather high. Hundreds, indeed." She snorted. "It can't be true."

"You have no idea, my dear. Three: this elevation in society not only gives you security, but it also assures you access to those ranks that you seek."

She frowned. "I don't follow. I don't have those kinds of aspirations at all."

"Then you ought. Let me put it this way. Who has more influence? A prim unmarried schoolmistress or a dashing duchess?"

She opened her mouth no doubt to say she was no prim schoolmistress but snapped her lips shut to ponder on the veracity of his claim.

"Fourthly. With said influence, you will easily acquire the funds, support, resources, etcetera, etcetera, that you need for building up England's most successful school. Not to disregard my fortune, which is immense. Fifthly. Is this even a word? You immediately gain the house you so crave."

Her eyes widened.

He smirked. Ah. She hadn't thought of the most obvious point, had she?

"It is evident, is it not? The two plots of land would be unified, all fences and boundaries fall. You can do with my house whatever you want. What's mine is yours."

"That is not correct," she quipped. "It would be the other way around. For upon marriage, all my property would become yours. I see no advantage at all from such a move. For everything I do, I would need your permission. I would have to give up my independence and my freedom. And who has ever heard of a duchess teaching in a schoolroom? It isn't done. Why on earth would I willingly put myself in such a position?"

"Because it is the only way for you to save your school."

"Explain."

"You are, of course, correct. By law, we men not only physically own the woman, but all she possesses. Dashedly convenient law for us men, is it not? However, never fear. I have never been that medieval. I pride myself to have a liberal mind and attitude, and we will draw up a marriage contract whereby you will keep your property and all your possessions. Including the house you so want. Consider it a marriage present. As for you asking my permission, we both know this is laughable, as you would never dream of asking my permission on anything. I rather fear it would be the other way around. Rest assured, you can do whatever you want for all I care. You can teach or not teach. It doesn't matter to me in the least. I certainly don't care a tuppence about what society thinks a duchess ought, or ought not, to be doing."

"Can you please answer me one question, honestly, and to the point?"

"By all means."

"Why?"

Why, indeed?

He felt they'd approached the moment of truth. He could tell a fib and answer flippantly and sarcastically, in his usual manner.

"What do you gain from all this?" she pressed.

He thought hard. One wrong word and he might lose it all. "Several things. Once more, you may tick them off mentally. Having a duchess is convenient as it keeps the persistent husband-hunters at bay."

"None of which has ever bothered you in the least."

"Secondly. Having gained a house in Bath, one might as well make use of it. Thirdly. It might be convenient to have a duchess here settling all my affairs while I haul myself away to India. You must admit that this is eminently practical. Fariq has seen to my affairs to a point, but the good man is up to his neck with his own business, and I don't trust solicitors. I have several estates, mansions, and whatnot. I have lost count. You could even set up a second school in one of those places."

Her eyes flew up to his. "India? You are planning on travelling soon?"

"Yes. The climate here doesn't agree with me. I have a passage booked and intend to leave in a month."

"I see." She lowered her head. "You are proposing a marriage of convenience. Where both parties, ultimately, are to do whatever they see fit."

"You have grasped the point of the matter," he replied cheerfully. "You would never even have to see my ugly visage. Convenient, don't you agree?"

She sighed.

"Or you could do the alternative."

Was that relief crossing her face? "That being?"

"We break off our sham marriage and face yet another scandal, nothing that is too unusual for me, for it would merely be...I have lost count...one of many scandals. A daily occurrence. You would have to weather through it somehow on your own and risk losing your reputation. They will drag up your old scandal, naturally, and the secretary of the Foundling Hospital might let slip a particularly juicy piece of gossip and that won't help things along. It is only a matter of time until he does. It won't do a thing to my already black reputation. People will shrug it away. But what about you?"

Eleonore swallowed.

The duke continued. "I will donate a fair share for the reconstruction of the school, but that is all that I can do in this scenario. In the worst case, you may have to change your name again and see whether that would help things along."

She was quiet.

"May I think about these options?" She sounded oddly humble in her request.

"By all means, but I don't think we have too much time left. The longer we allow this to go on, the more complicated things get."

The waltz had ended.

He let her go, and his arms felt oddly empty. Was it his imagination or was the ballroom suddenly chilly? It had been overheated before.

She nodded. "This is a decision that needs some serious thought. I do not want this to be precipitous."

Later, as he disappeared into the card room, he acknowledged he hadn't been truthful in a single thing he'd said.

Why hadn't he?

Because the answer had been very simple.

He needed her more than he needed air to breathe.

So, he'd conceived a brilliant plan: marry her.

Make her his.

Then get away from her, fast.

It was a good plan.

It was an excellent plan.

It made perfect sense to his convoluted mind.

CHAPTER TWENTY-ONE

Saturday evening

Lady Blackwater gave a grand ball and supper at her house in Grosvenor Squ. The rooms were beautifully decorated with garlands in Lady Blackwater's most superior taste; the supper tables were covered with this season's exquisite delicacies. The ball was opened by Lord and Lady Norfolk. A wide range of illustrious guests attended the ball. Great interest and speculation were aroused by the attendance of the newly married Duke and Duchess of Rochford, for many a debutante is still in mourning over the sudden and unexpected loss of this season's prime catch...

Miss Eleonore Hilversham, also known as Miss Violetta Winford, daughter of the late Lord Leighton, was attending her very first ball at age thirty-five and no one could tell.

That was quite a feat.

It was quite ironic, too, for dancing and ballroom etiquette were on her school's curriculum. She'd hired a dancing master who came once a week to her school to teach her students country dances, quadrilles, the cotillion, and the waltz. Once a year, she rented the local ballroom and invited the boys' school in the neighbourhood. It was the highlight of the year for both students and teachers. She'd been at those balls as the organiser and watched everyone else dance from the side. But she'd never attended any such event as a debutante herself since she never had a proper coming out, as was customary for a young lady of her class.

So, when her mother had suggested they go to the Blackwater ball together, she'd been terrified.

But then a sense of excitement had taken hold of her, and she'd felt like a young girl again. Not only was her ballroom gown gorgeous, but her matching embroidered slippers were also the prettiest shoes she'd ever worn. Her hair, which she normally disliked, looked elegant in a chignon, with some loose strands curling against her nape.

When she saw Rochford waiting for her at the bottom of the stairs, she'd nearly gasped.

Used to seeing him in semi-deshabille, she barely recognised him in full, formal evening gear. She'd only ever seen him in his dishevelled state, his chin and cheeks covered by stubble.

He was dressed in an elegant black tailcoat of impeccable cut with silver buttons, a crisp white cravat, and buckled shoes. For once, he was cleanly shaven, and his chin, without the sprinkling of stubble, was firm; his full lips curled into a faintly satirical smile. His keen, green eyes were fringed by thick, dark lashes. She'd swallowed heavily and fanned herself.

No wonder the women were consistently after him.

She also found herself in an odd role.

People thought she was his duchess.

The ball had started promising enough. Their quarrelling caught some attention, but Eleonore had to admit she enjoyed those spats as much as he. By now she knew she ought not to take half of the things he said seriously. How could she ever have missed that teasing gleam in his eyes whenever he called her "prim"? That delighted expression that crossed his face every time she picked up the gauntlet, as she did every single time, for she could not resist.

Then he'd proposed in the middle of the waltz.

Turn the pretence into reality. He had seemed earnest about the suggestion.

She fanned herself slowly as she watched his tall figure disappear into the card room.

He'd said some truths there. A marriage to a duke, no matter how disastrous his reputation, would be an advantage. Duke was duke. Those on top of the hierarchy could get away with breaking the rules, whereas those on the bottom couldn't. If they called off the engagement, it would barely hurt him, but they would dig out her old, long-forgotten scandals, and a ruined schoolmistress carried very little moral weight. Everything she'd built up would be in jeopardy.

She sighed.

She'd been so careful all these years. She thought she'd rebuilt her existence successfully. Had she built everything on quicksand? Was that the life she wanted to lead: a tenuous one, consistently fearing exposure?

She got on her feet, snapped her fan shut, and went after Marcus in the card room.

Little groups of men gathered around the tables in the room. The biggest group, by far, was the one where Marcus was. He leaned back in his chair, an expression of utter boredom on his face as he played out his cards.

This was another thing about him that puzzled her. Why was he gambling if he did not enjoy it?

The footman offered him a tray with champagne, but he waved it away.

She stepped next to him and reached out to touch his sleeve for his attention.

"Your wife, Rochford?" His partner glanced up with a gleam of interest in his eyes.

"Eleonore." Rochford set down his cards.

His partner pushed his cards away. "I never would've thought I'd see the day that Rochford, of all people, enters the harbour of matrimony." He leaned forward. "It was a rather sudden decision, was it not?"

Rochford shrugged. "I see no point in dragging things out."

The man laughed. "You are entirely right, Your Grace." He nodded at Eleonore. "I knew your godmother, Lady Adkins, rather well in her time."

Eleonore recognised him. "Lord Cameron. I remember. You were one of Madelyn's regular visitors."

"Ah, the good old times. I must say, no one has ever been able to step into your godmother's shoes." Lord Cameron stood up. "How times have changed." He bowed and left.

Marcus made a motion with his hand for her to sit.

Eleonore sat.

He looked at her through hooded eyes. "Care to play against the most skilful gambler in all of London?"

"Oh, very well. You will fleece me shamefully, so I might as well give it a try."

He shuffled the cards and distributed them.

"Were you winning against Lord Cameron?"

He placed a card face down. "Naturally. You go first."

She studied her cards and chose one randomly. Eleonore never played, and she dared not admit she barely knew the rules of vingt-et-un. She would simply pretend she knew what she was doing.

"Do you still love him?" he asked out of the blue.

She blinked at him. "Who? Lord Cameron?"

He twitched his lips. "No. Edward Lawrence, of course."

How to answer that? She could barely remember what she'd seen in him. The truth was that she'd been infatuated with Edward, that in her headstrongness she hadn't seen the weaker sides of his personality. He'd been petty and had a streak towards cruelty, but she'd been so besotted and blinded by his attention to her.

Marcus watched her closely and barely looked at his cards when he chose and played out a random card.

"I was only sixteen. I hardly understood love." She thought she'd loved him, but he'd taken advantage of her innocence and seduced her.

"If he were alive, I'd shoot a bullet into him," Marcus growled.

"Unnecessary," Eleonore said lightly. "He died in the war."

She played out another card.

"You are rather hideous at this game. Are you sure you know the rules?" Marcus asked as he won the next round.

She lifted her chin. "I am a schoolmistress, not a gambler. I am, naturally, improvising."

He grinned at her honesty.

It was her turn to ask. "Do you still love her?" Her heart hammered against her ribs. There was no question at all about who she meant.

"Yes." His answer came without hesitation.

She felt her heart pummel into the depths of the earth.

"In the manner one loves the memory of a dream," he added after a moment of silence. "A fantasy that takes hold of one's mind like a fever." He put down his cards. "I was maybe not as innocent as you, but still a boy when it happened. I had no defences. I've been licking my wounds ever since."

"What a pair we are," Eleonore whispered.

They played on in silence.

"Marcus?"

"Hm?"

"We are friends, are we not?" She sounded like a timid child.

She thought at first that he wouldn't reply. When he did, it sounded more like a grunt. "Hm. I suppose so." Then he leaned back and assessed her. He flashed a smile at her that was so unexpected that it took her breath away. It wasn't one of his sarcastic smiles, but a genuine one, coming from the depths of his being. "Another round?"

"No. I don't want to play." She pleated the fabric of her

gown between her fingers. "I just wanted to tell you that I have made my decision."

He stilled.

Eleonore moistened her lips. "I have decided to accept your proposal. I will marry you for real."

His fingers tensed around his cards. "Are you certain?"

"Yes."

"Tomorrow."

"Tomorrow." She blinked. "Already?"

"To get it done and over with. A quiet wedding in a quiet church. No one will know about it. We'll be spared the drama of a big wedding and time-wise it would be convenient, too. I can take an earlier passage to India, and you can return to your beloved school."

His words punched her in the gut. "India. Of course." He would marry her quickly and leave her. Her life would continue as before, except now she'd be wealthier and have a title. He couldn't have made it clearer that he did not care a whit about her.

Then why would he do this? Why go through the trouble of marrying her? What had he to gain?

Maybe he was right. The sooner she got this done and over with, the better. She could not wait to return to Bath.

She felt her heart thump in her chest and wondered why it pained her so.

His keen green eyes were intent on her.

She exhaled a shaky breath. "Very well. Tomorrow."

CHAPTER TWENTY-TWO

MATRIMONY
Yesterday was married, at St Philip's church, by the Rev John
Morton, the Duke of Rochford to Miss Hilversham, Bath.

*M*arcus tugged at his cravat and wished it to the devil. His valet had tied it tightly, according to the latest cry. If he could have had his way, he'd have married in his beloved morning gown, but he supposed that wasn't quite the thing to wear at his wedding. He also felt that his waistcoat was too tight. He must've gained weight; otherwise, it was inexplicable why breathing was so difficult. His breath was shallow, and he felt somewhat lightheaded. He drummed his fingers against the worm-eaten wood of the pew.

The bride hadn't appeared yet.

The parish priest was waiting patiently in front of the

altar, folding his hands in front of him as if he were praying.

Fariq was sitting next to Marcus, fidgeting. Why on earth was the boy nervous? It wasn't as though as he was putting his head into the noose.

They were in an insignificant little church in the outer districts of London. No one would know them here, and the priest had shown himself to be uncomplicated in transacting this rather rushed marriage. The second witness was his coach driver, John.

"Do you think I'm making a mistake?" Marcus asked abruptly.

Fariq stopped tapping his foot on the stone floor. "Of course."

Marcus grumbled.

"Getting married is always a mistake. Isn't that what you've always preached?"

He may have a point. His entire life had been focused with incredible energy at avoiding marriage. So why was he shackling himself now?

"There is still time to run," Fariq offered. "It's what you always do, isn't it?"

Marcus sat up straight. "Who do you think I am?"

Fariq grinned. "You are the wicked duke who'd never shackle himself, especially not to a sharp-tongued spinster."

Marcus scowled. "She's about to become my duchess, so you'd better watch your words."

Fariq studied his finely polished fingernails. "Unless, of course, you've undergone a profound change of personality. Which I think is unlikely. This leaves only one explanation."

"Which is?"

"You've fallen in love." Fariq ducked.

Marcus felt tempted to slam his fist into his grinning face.

The reverend cleared his throat.

Footsteps echoed.

She had arrived.

She was wearing a midnight-blue empire day dress with long sleeves and a high neckline laced with a slight ruff. A warm golden Kashmir shawl was draped over her arms. It was the only present she'd ever received from Marcus. When she'd tried to return it, he'd said, gruffly, that she could keep it.

He'd never seen a more beautiful woman.

Marcus suppressed a curse. Things must be in a sad state with him, indeed; for when the deuce had he begun thinking of her as beautiful?

She nodded at them. "You may begin," she told the reverend coolly.

The reverend rattled off the words unceremoniously. When he reached the crucial passage, Marcus held his breath.

"I will," she replied. It didn't sound frightful or timid. But determined. She lifted her eyes and met his.

When the reverend posed the crucial question, he knew without a doubt that what he was going to do was about to change his life forever.

The answer came across his lips easily. "I will."

The earth didn't shake; the ground didn't open, and the ceiling didn't collapse. Neither did a thunderbolt strike him down. The contrary happened. He felt something lift. An age-old burden.

He'd never felt so light before. He felt, for the first time in his life, that he'd never said or done anything so sane.

"I will," he repeated, grinning foolishly at his new wife.

He might have repeated the word a third time, just to test whether it still felt as good, when the reverend cleared his throat. "Well then, kiss your wife and sign the papers."

Fariq suppressed a snort.

Eleonore's corners of her mouth twitched. He planted a quick, sweet kiss on her upturned lips. There would be time for more later.

HE WAS MARRIED.

Outside the church, the world still revolved around its axis.

He was married.

The sun was still shining; the children were still playing in the streets. He blinked his eyes against the sudden bright sunlight.

The coach was waiting.

It occurred to him that he'd made no plans. Traditionally, there would be a wedding breakfast somewhere. He'd forgotten all about it. One could take the bride to his home and start the wedding night in plain daylight, he mused. Then he remembered he hadn't even notified the servants that they were to have a duchess. They probably needed some time to get things ready.

Fariq came to the rescue, as always. "Your Grace, and Your Grace," he bowed ceremoniously to both. He produced a gigantic bouquet and handed it to Eleonore. "May I be the first to congratulate?"

Flowers. Of course. Leave it up to Fariq to think of everything.

"Thank you, Fariq." Eleonore blinked her eyes rapidly as she took the bouquet. Maybe it was just the sun glinting against her spectacles.

"Unless you have anything else planned, I suggest that we have a wedding breakfast at the Perpignol. You can eat in peace there."

Marcus clapped him on the shoulder. "Splendid plan, old chap."

"But before we do that," Fariq rubbed his hands, "I suggest we attend another event."

"Which event? I am not in the mood for any socialising. The whole point of this affair was to keep it quiet."

"Never fear. No one will notice you. You will stand on the sidelines and watch."

"And why would we do that?"

Fariq shook his head back and forth. "Trust me on this. Her Grace would find it profoundly interesting."

"What is it, Fariq?" Eleonore looked up from her flowers.

"I thought it might be the thing to watch your daughter get married," Fariq dusted an invisible speck off his sleeve.

CHAPTER TWENTY-THREE

MATRIMONY

Mr Robert Lexter, Oxford, to Miss Rosalie Weston, daughter of Mr Francis Weston, Industrialist, Marylebone, London, At St James's church, by the Rev George Wright

$\mathcal{E}$leonore's legs gave way, and she nearly collapsed on the street. Marcus caught her at the last moment.

She felt light-headed and dizzy. "This is not a joking matter." Her voice wobbled.

"It is not a joke. I have found your daughter." Fariq insisted.

"Couldn't you have come up with a less dramatic way to announce this?" Marcus said testily.

"I thought it was a nice wedding present. Also, the coincidence is interesting, wouldn't you say? Your daughter getting married on the same day as you."

"How...where...who...?" She couldn't even form a coherent sentence.

"If it would behove Your Graces to get into the carriage, I can explain everything on the way to St James. We must hurry if you don't want to miss it."

"St James." Eleonore grabbed Marcus' hand and found that her entire body trembled.

In the carriage, Fariq told them the story.

"It was surprisingly easy to find your daughter." Fariq hooked both thumbs into the breast pockets of his waistcoat. "After I received your missive, I could not resist being drawn into the mystery of the missing child. I knew there would be a logical explanation."

"Pray cut out any long preambles and get to the point. Who is she, where is she, and who is she marrying?"

"Patience is a virtue, Your Grace." Fariq leaned back with a smug smirk. "But to answer the basics: her name is Rosalie Weston, and she is about to marry a Mr Robert Lexter."

"Rosalie," Eleonore whispered. The name sounded foreign on her lips.

"Here are the facts." He ticked them off on his fingers. "In the missive, you wrote that Molly Barton, your mother's maid, took the baby to the Foundling Hospital eighteen years ago. Your mother chose Molly because she was a discreet servant and loyal to the family. She would not breathe a word to anyone. There was no reason to doubt her veracity. She told your mother that she'd drawn the white ball at the ballot and that the child was admitted. However, there are no records of the child in the admission books. Am I correct?"

"Yes." Eleonore's voice was hoarse.

"The conclusion is clear: Molly never took the child there." Marcus drummed his fingers against the carriage seat.

Eleonore plucked the crimson petals of her bouquet. They dropped on the floor like drops of blood. "That is what I feared."

"Let me continue." Fariq flexed his fingers. "The thing is that you have been looking at the wrong register. You have been looking at the admittance register. But not the ballot register. The ballot register does have a record of Molly Barton being invited to the ballot on August 15. There is a checkmark next to the names of mothers who drew a white ball, meaning their child was admitted. "Black ball" is scribbled next to those who were declined. But next to Molly Barton's name, there is a line. Nothing."

"Well done, Fariq. This is evidence that she never went to the ballot." Marcus shot him an approving look.

"This much seems certain. Then something interesting happened. Several days later, Molly suddenly resigned from your parents' service. After twenty years of loyal service, she leaves. Just like that. That is certainly strange, wouldn't you agree? Well, you may not be surprised that I have discovered that she is now living affluently in Reading, married, and owner of a haberdashery. Business is going well."

"What are you saying? I don't understand." Eleonore crushed the stems of the bouquet.

"I do." Marcus put in. "The crucial question being where she acquired the money."

Eleonore felt all her blood drain from her face. "No. You're not implying she sold my baby?"

"I am afraid I am," Fariq said. "But she would never see it in those terms."

"Continue." Marcus placed his hand on her arm.

"Turns out, Molly Barton had every intention of taking the child to the hospital. On the way there, she met a childhood friend from her village who was in service as well. That friend, let's call her Peggy, was working for a well-to-do family. The Westons are industrialists, something to do with textiles. Peggy was close to her mistress, who had everything she wanted. A husband who doted on her, a beautiful house, clothes, and jewellery …."

"But not a child." Eleonore's eyes burned.

"But not a child." Fariq nodded.

"Peggy persuaded Molly to take the child to her mistress, Mrs Weston, who, it turns out, had every intention of adopting a child from the Foundling Hospital. The baby Molly was about to take to the Hospital was healthy and up for adoption. Why go through the bureaucracy? She decided to keep it."

"Just like that," Eleonore gasped.

"Just like that."

Fariq continued. "Molly, of course, was given ample compensation from the Westons for keeping quiet. She returned to your father's estate to quit service, for why remain in service when you now have the means to be independent? And Lady Leighton, your mother, having no reason to distrust Molly, never suspected any of this."

The carriage was quiet, save for the rattling of the wheels and the clapping of the horseshoes.

Eleonore's hand shook as she wiped her cheeks. "How did you discover all this?"

"It was easy. I used to be a servant once." He looked

askance at the duke. "Servants talk to other servants. There isn't a bigger grapevine. Everyone knows everything about each other's masters. Who works where, why, and for how long. Which master is good, who is not, and where one wouldn't want to work at any cost. What positions are available and where one ought to apply? And where not? Not to mention all the gossip and rumours."

Marcus growled. "You're saying there's a tremendous network of spies that exchange information on everything we do, from what we eat to how often we piss in the chamber pot. And that my butler, footmen, valet, and you are all part of it."

"You have understood the gist of the matter." Fariq beamed. "How else would I have uncovered this information so quickly? I also sent a bow street runner to Reading, of course."

The carriage arrived in front of St James, where traffic was heavy, no doubt because of the wedding.

"The plan is to go inside and to sit in the back pews and pretend to be a wedding guest. No one will recognise you if you go about this circumspectly." Fariq held out a hand to help Eleonore down from the carriage, but she lifted her skirts and jumped down without his help.

The church inside was packed full.

At the front of the altar, a couple stood in front of a priest.

They were too far away. She would not see a thing if she remained in the back.

Since quite a few people were standing by the side, it did not appear unusual that she remained standing as well.

She sidled as close as she could to the front, trying to glimpse her daughter's face.

She was dressed in a light blue gown and wore a bonnet. She was slim, of medium height, but the bonnet shaded her face.

They said their vows.

Then she turned and lifted her face, and oh!

Her daughter was beautiful. Her nose was finely chiselled, her wide mouth curving into a smile. She was brimming with joy.

And her eyes, which lit up, had the same colour as hers.

Everyone got up and clapped.

The wedding was over.

The couple moved down the aisle. The bride stopped, and a tall, well-dressed woman broke from the crowd and hugged her fiercely.

A gentleman with grey hair stepped up to them, cleared his throat, and made one, two awkward movements before throwing his hesitation to the wind. He hugged both women. Then he hugged the bridegroom, his daughter, and his wife. And then they were all hugging each other.

Eleonore had never seen so much hugging before.

"Today, ladies and gentlemen," the elderly gentleman, who must be Mr Weston, said, "today is a good day. My wonderful daughter, the apple of my eye, the child of my heart, has married an equally wonderful, bright young man." He clapped the bridegroom on the shoulder.

"Hear, hear," voices said.

"Keep the speech for the wedding breakfast!" advised another.

A general round of laughter followed.

"Yes. To the wedding breakfast we go. Today we will celebrate all day."

The couple moved down the aisle, followed by her parents and the remaining wedding guests. The church emptied.

Eleonore collapsed in a pew.

Someone sat next to her.

"She—she was so happy." Eleonore lifted her eyes and met Marcus's green ones. "Not only marrying the man she evidently loves but also—her parents."

"They seem to be decent people," Marcus observed. "Your daughter seems to have been very lucky."

Eleonore picked up a rose that was left on the pew. She stared at it. Then tears poured forth, and she dropped the flower on the floor.

A pair of arms clamped about her shoulders as she wept.

After a while, she wiped her face and cleaned her nose with a handkerchief, pulled back her shoulders, and said, "Let us go."

She blinked as she stepped from the church out into the bright sunlight.

She had seen her daughter.

She was beautiful.

She was loved.

She also had her eyes.

And they had both married on the same day.

Eleonore looked at Marcus with surprise. She'd entirely forgotten that he was her husband now. What a thought to get used to.

In the carriage, she sat up with a jerk. "Marcus! Something occurred to me."

"What?"

"My daughter just got married." She laughed.

Fariq and Marcus exchanged worried glances.

"That means I am a mother-in-law," she said in between two giggles.

"Reasonable conclusion," Fariq contributed.

"That also means that you have married a soon-to-be grandmother. Imagine that. We could be grandparents soon."

She folded her hands, satisfied at the disconcerted expression on Marcus's face. "By Jove! You may be right."

Fariq slapped his thighs in delight.

CHAPTER TWENTY-FOUR

FOR PASSENGERS ONLY
The following ships, belonging to the East India Company, are
scheduled to depart from the East India Docks on Dec 2nd: The
Lord Melville, outward bound for Calcutta; The Asia and the
Admiral Blanket for Bengal...

They had to pretend like nothing at all had happened.

That she hadn't just seen her beautiful daughter.

That she hadn't just married.

It was odd not being able to tell anyone that she'd just married the Duke of Rochford, for everyone believed she was already married to him. On some level that made things easier, and they were spared long strings of congratulations, speeches, and other events.

On the other hand, it was strange that life seemed to continue as before.

The bouquet that Fariq had given her and that Eleonore had arranged in a vase in the drawing room was the only proof that this morning's events hadn't been a dream. They had returned to her townhouse, where her mother had awaited them. Marcus had muttered something about Rochford House not being ready yet, and her mother had accepted that without blinking.

When her mother came into the drawing room, chattering away about inconsequential things, she decided to do things differently.

"Mother, I need to tell you something."

She invited her mother to sit and told her everything. About her daughter. About her marriage to Rochford. About how nothing had been planned.

Her mother nodded. Once or twice, she wiped a tear from the corner of her eye. Then she got up and embraced Eleonore. "I am glad," she said. "So glad."

That was all.

THE DAYS AFTER THEIR WEDDING, SHE SAW VERY LITTLE OF Marcus. Now that they were married, it seemed he was putting all his energy into staying away from her as if she had cholera, the plague, and the pox combined. They had not even had a proper wedding night. He'd merely patted her arm in an avuncular fashion and sent her to her room, insisting she needed to rest. She disliked that hearty, slightly patronising demeanour he'd adopted towards her since their marriage. It was an entirely new side to him. If he called her "my dear" one more time in that falsely amicable way, as if he were her uncle and not her husband, she would bash one of his Indian vases over his head. What had happened to the arrogant, ill-mannered boor? Not that it mattered, because most of the time he was not at home.

When she woke up in the morning, he was already out. He'd missed supper and returned only after she was already asleep. That went on for several days. She informed the butler that he was to tell her immediately the moment her husband set foot in the house.

Eleonore lurked in the hallway and pounced on him as soon as he stepped into the foyer.

"There you are." She grabbed his arm and pulled him into the drawing room before he could utter 'good afternoon.' "We are going to have tea now. Together. Like a properly married couple. Sit." She pushed him into a chair.

"Yes, ma'am," he replied meekly.

She placed a scone, a cress sandwich, and a piece of seed cake on his plate and poured him a cup of masala chai.

"Drink. Eat." She stood in front of him, her hands on her hips.

He shrank in his seat. "Yes, ma'am."

"Stop saying yes, ma'am."

"Yes—ma'am." He took a timid sip from his cup.

Eleonore glared at him.

He raised his hand. "Excuse the question, miss school-teacher. But did I do something wrong?"

Eleonore was about to open her mouth and pour forth a tirade about his execrable behaviour when the butler entered with a tray bearing a big envelope. "The mail, Your Grace."

Marcus took it, opened it, and laid it aside without a word.

Eleonore glanced at it and felt a chill go through her body.

It came from *The East India Company*.

"What are your plans now?" Eleonore shoved the cress that had fallen out of her sandwich back and forth on her plate.

"Plans?" He stirred another heaped spoonful of sugar into his tea. It was a miracle his spoon didn't get stuck in a pile of undissolved sugar. "I might go to the club and meet Fariq in the Perpignol afterwards. Your brother's rather taken with me, too. Wants me to teach him all my card tricks. He's insatiable."

"No. I mean, with regards to that." She pointed at the envelope that lay on the table. "Is this your passage?"

He stared at it. "It appears it is," he said after a brief pause.

"It *appears*?" Her voice sounded sharp.

"Wrong word? I'd almost forgotten that one has to be particular about choosing the appropriate vocabulary when conversing with you."

Eleonore hissed.

Marcus looked up, pleased. "I'd forgotten you could do that, Miss Puss."

"Don't digress. You intend to take yourself off so immediately after our marriage. I assumed you'd be post-poning, if not cancelling, the trip."

"Postponing? Cancelling? Why?"

She formed her hands into fists so that her fingernails bit into her palms. Heaven help her. Conversing with him was like talking with a thick-headed schoolboy. Yet he was correct, wasn't he? That had been their understanding, hadn't it? That each would go about their separate ways; she would return to her school, and he would pretend he'd never even married. She'd just thought—with everything that had happened—that things would be different now.

Since he was sipping his tea without a care in the world and bent on pursuing his original plan, it appeared she'd drawn the wrong conclusion.

"I see." She straightened her back. "I have been under the impression—" she lifted a hand to wave her words away. "Never mind. I was wrong. Of course, do whatever you want, even if that means travelling to India not three days after our marriage. I will, in turn, pack my bags and return to Bath. I am wasting my time here. There is much work there, and my teachers are waiting for me." Her voice was steely.

He studied the little glass bowl with the clotted cream as if it were the most interesting thing in the world. "Bath. So you should, my dear."

"There is much work to do. Ellen Robinson has sent me daily missives about the school's development, and my presence is needed there now as never."

"Naturally, my dear."

She clutched her butter knife. "Stop calling me 'my dear.' I will leave tomorrow."

"Tomorrow already?" He threw her a quick look. "I thought—Never mind, never mind. Have a pleasant trip, then, my d—." he cleared his throat. "I will be leaving for the club and am most definitely not capable of getting up before noon. My ship departs a day later in the morning."

She would rather die than see him off. She would not

247

remain on the pier and wave a handkerchief as his ship disappeared on the horizon. Not her.

"Have a good trip, Your Grace. I suppose we will see each other in several years."

She left the room, her head held high, while he remained behind, buttering his scone with concentration.

CHAPTER TWENTY-FIVE

SEMINARY REOPENING
Miss Hilversham respectfully informs her friends and the public
that her NEW SEMINARY for Young Ladies in BATH will
reopen on September 1ˢᵗ.

$\mathcal{I}$t was summer again, and the construction of the school had advanced nicely. The foundations were standing. The roof had been rebuilt. It was all thanks to Fariq, who supervised the construction site regularly, and who knew how to find the best workers in town.

"There's been good progress," Ellen said after she'd returned. "No doubt it helps that you are a duchess now, Your Grace. I must add that none of us was surprised when we heard the news."

Had the entire world known she was going to marry

Marcus? She merely smiled at Ellen and refrained from commenting.

"The duke's design is genius," Ellen said. "It will be a spacious school with all the necessary facilities, without appearing like an institution without a soul. The duke has a feeling for the aesthetics of the place. It will be a beautiful school."

Eleonore agreed. They had used Marcus's architectural design, which she had liked at first sight. She had to admit that her original plan of transforming the wishing well house into the main school would have been only half as impressive.

Fariq had arrived not a week after she'd returned to Bath.

"Marcus has left," was all he'd said with sympathy in his eyes.

Eleonore had pressed her lips together.

It was better this way.

If only she could get over the gawping hole that was now in her heart.

LIFE HAD SUDDENLY BECOME VERY BUSY. AS THE DUCHESS of Rochford, she received countless invitations to soirees, balls, and dinners, which she turned down regularly. She was far too busy.

She'd thrown heart and soul into her school construction project, sitting up late until the candle burned down to a blob of wax. She spent much time collecting and buying books and asking various people for donations, for books were rare and expensive. Her dream was to create a library that was even bigger than before. She visited London frequently, staying with her mother or at the gloomy Rochford mansion, which was supposed to be her home now, too.

Her mother visited her frequently in Bath. She helped pick out wallpaper, curtains and carpets. She'd thrown herself into the project with as much enthusiasm as Eleonore.

"I missed out on helping you the first time around," her mother provided as an explanation.

Eleonore was glad to have her mother with her. They had much to catch up on. So much lost time.

Ned visited frequently with his new wife, Esther. She was expecting a child soon. Eleonore was to be an aunt! She was happy, yet her thoughts strayed to her daughter with a tinge of sadness.

She sent out advertisements for new teachers, and her time was filled with interviewing people who applied for the job. It was as difficult as always. Alas, most applicants were not suitable at all. Miss Everglade and Miss Johnson had returned, but she still needed a new music master, a new history teacher, and a Latin teacher.

Eleonore buried herself in her work. She would do anything to keep herself from thinking.

But at night, when she tossed and turned, her thoughts were far away over the ocean. She followed him, then. He would be at the Cape of Good Hope. Then on to Madagascar. Then on to India...

Of course, he wasn't writing.

Not him.

ONE MORNING, MARTHA INTERRUPTED HER IN THE MIDDLE of work.

"There's someone to see you, ma'am."

They received few visitors lately. Eleonore wiped the ink from her fingers and wondered who it might be.

When she stepped into the drawing room, everything inside her froze.

A young woman rose from the sofa, slim, lithe, with light blonde hair and silver eyes. She was dressed in a green travelling gown and a fichu, fiddling with the strings on her bonnet.

"Miss Hilversham?" she asked after a moment's hesitation.

Eleonore's mouth dried out. She clasped the edge of the table for support. "Yes."

"I am Rosalie Lexter."

Hope, she felt tempted to reply. You're Hope. But not a word came across her lips.

Hadn't she always wished for this? For her daughter to step across her doorstep? For her child to appear. She'd thrown a coin in the wishing well for this. It seemed surreal, hardly possible that it was happening.

"I was wondering whether it was too early to enrol my child in the school." The woman looked at her uneasily.

"What child?" Eleonore's eyes looked around for a child in the room she might have missed.

Rosalie smiled vaguely and placed a hand on her stomach. "She is not yet born."

"I—see." Eleonore dropped into her chair. "Please. If you would have a seat."

The young woman sat again. "I have heard so much about your school," she burst out. "It is the best school in

England, and I have heard so much about you. I have always wanted to go to a school like yours. Because I didn't, I want to make sure that my child can."

"How do you know it will be a girl? What if it is a boy?"

"Do you not take boys?"

"It is a girl's school, Seminary for Young Ladies."

"Oh. Of course." The young woman fiddled around with her scarf. "Could I inscribe her anyhow? Just in case she will be a girl?" Her voice was pleading.

Eleonore mechanically pulled out a sheet of paper and a quill. "How would you call her if she were a girl?"

The young woman smiled. "We don't know yet for sure. Robert wants her to be Georgette. But I think I want her to be—" she hesitated.

"Yes?"

"Eleonore." She whispered.

The quill fell from Eleonore's trembling fingers.

There was not a sound in the room save for the ticking of the ormolu on the mantlepiece.

Rosalie fumbled in her reticule and pulled out a trinket. It was a round, silver trinket, similar to what she had.

"I have had this ever since I was a baby. My parents never made a secret of the fact that they'd adopted me, and they said this was the trinket which was given to me. Do you know what it contains?"

"A lock of silver-blonde hair," Eleonore whispered.

"Yes." Rosalie's face was as white as Eleonore's. "I used to look at it all the time, wondering about my birth mother. At the same time, I loved and still love my parents with all my heart. I was and still am, very close to my mother. I count myself lucky to have such wonderful parents."

Eleonore felt herself nod.

"The other day, when I pulled it out, wondering what my birth mother would say when she found out that I married, wondering whether she even cared, it slipped from my fingers and dropped to the ground. It opened and revealed a second chamber inside that I did not know existed." She ran her tongue over her dry lips. "Inside is a crest. The crest of the Leighton family. We visited Baron Leighton, who was friendly, but he would not give me very much information at all. He said the answers I was seeking were here. With Miss Eleonore Hilversham in Bath. Was he correct? Will I find the answers here, Miss Hilversham?"

Eleonore's hand crept to her mouth. Then she nodded. "It is very much possible. It is likely. I believe–you are my daughter." Her voice broke.

Both women rose together.

Both women stared at each other.

Then they were in each other's arms, weeping.

WHAT A MIRACLE, ELEONORE THOUGHT AS SHE WENT TO bed that night. Not in a million years had she imagined that she would ever meet her daughter. They had talked, gazed at each other, and talked again. Eleonore had told her they had married on the same day, and that she had been present at her wedding.

They parted on the understanding that Eleonore was to call on her when she was in London next.

"It is a miracle," Eleonore kept repeating to herself.

Dazed, she went to bed, and could not sleep.

The full moon was out, and the night sky was clear.

It was on a night like this that she'd gone to the wishing well and Fariq had clubbed her over the head.

Eleonore smiled and involuntarily touched the back of her head. The bump had disappeared within a few days.

If only she could tell Marcus she had finally found her daughter. Or, rather, that her daughter had found her. The wishing well does make wishes come true, she thought.

Eleonore got up, grabbed her Kashmir shawl, and went out into the garden. She walked to the wishing well, remembering the night he'd kissed her. It hadn't been for the first time. But it had been the most magical time.

She stared down the well, seeing the stars reflected in the black water.

"Are you sleepwalking or trying to drown yourself? Or both?" A male voice said behind her.

She whirled around with a shriek.

"Not sleepwalking." He stood in front of her as if grown from the ground. "I knew I'd find you here."

"Marcus." She pressed her hand against her heart. "It cannot be." She closed her eyes and opened them again, but he was still there. "What on earth are you doing here?"

He caught her by the arms. "The thing is this. I took the ship to India, thinking it was what I had to do. I've been wanting to go to India for a while, you see. It's an itch, a restlessness that won't be quenched unless I act on it. And usually, it works."

"Running away, you mean." Her voice came out thinly.

He ran a hand through his hair. "Running away. It's a speciality of mine. I used to think it solves my problems, you see. Then an odd thing happened. It all got worse. The restlessness, the dreams, the sleepless nights. It was unbearable. The ship was too tight, and I was seasick most of the time." He sat down at the edge of the well and pulled her onto his lap.

"How uncomfortable." She curled into him and inhaled his musky smell as if fearing he'd disappear again.

"Yes. I'd forgotten how much I hate being on a ship. Do you know who I dreamed of when I finally could sleep?"

She sighed. "Of course. Adika."

He shook his head. "They were about you. You, alone. And the nightmares were all the same. You were in that house—" he nodded at the new school, "and it burned, and you were inside. I shouted, I cried, I hollered, but I couldn't reach you."

She felt a knot in her throat.

"And so, when the ship docked at the Cape of Good Hope, I decided to blazes with it all. I jumped onto the returning ship to England. I needed to get back. To you." His eyes burned into hers. "I arrived here in Bath only a few moments ago and headed directly for the garden. On a night like this, you would be out here by the well."

"Oh, Marcus. It has been such a magical day for me. Do you know my daughter came here this afternoon? All this time, she has searched for me. I have finally held my daughter in my arms, Marcus." She wept. "And you have returned the same day. Can it be true?"

He uttered an oath and pulled her into his arms, his lips crushing hers. "I have been a fool to think I could ever leave you. I believed I could outrun it. But you're in my blood. You're the air that I breathe. I can't live without it. I can't live without you. Can you ever forgive me?"

She lifted her hand and touched his cheek, which was covered with stubble, and gave him another kiss as an answer.

"I am tired of running. I would like to stay with you if you will have this miserable, boorish, ill-mannered lout that I am. And I will try everything in my might to make you happy. I will help you build up that infernal school. I want to see it grow, and I want to see you preside over it all. I never want to be parted from you again. And if I ever return to India, it will be only with you on a late honeymoon. What do you say?" He lifted her in his arms and turned to carry her back to the house.

Her heart soared.

"With all my heart."

EPILOGUE

INVITATION

*The Joyous occasion of the reopening of Miss Hilversham's
Seminary for Young Ladies will be celebrated with a gala
festivity, including bountiful entertainment, performances of
music and theatre, dancing, and more.*

*E*veryone had come.

The Dukes and Duchesses of Ashmore,
Dunross, and Morley. The Earl of Halsford and his wife,
Frances. The parents and guardians of her current
students, and the entire neighbourhood as well, since they
had been so supportive after the school had burned down.
Champagne bottles popped, and liveried footmen passed
around silver trays with little marzipan cakes, strawber-
ries dipped in chocolate, candied almonds and sugar
plums.

Today was the grand opening of Miss Hilversham's New Seminary for Young Ladies. The new school building was imposing, built with a creamy stately façade, four classical columns in the front, and a driveway. The hedges between the two properties were gone; and on the sweeping meadow were tents with tables loaded with drinks, sweets, and sandwiches. A string orchestra played, and there was even some dancing. The house was open for tours.

Eleonore was radiant. Her cheeks were flushed, her eyes sparkled, and there was an overall softness about the Duchess of Rochford that the starchy Miss Hilversham had lacked.

"May I ask something?" Fariq asked after he'd sauntered over and lifted his champagne glass to Eleonore as a greeting. "Why do you still call it Miss Hilversham's Seminary? And not the Duchess of Rochford's Seminary? The latter has more of a regal ring to it, wouldn't you say?"

"Oh, but impossible," Lucy, the Duchess of Ashmore, replied, who'd overheard him. "It has to be Miss Hilversham's Seminary because she is the soul of the school. Miss Hilversham is an institution on her own, you know."

"Quite right," Halsford, who stood nearby, said. "It wouldn't be the same school under another name."

"Halsford, also known as the painter Tiverton, has painted us a new mural. It is spectacular," Eleonore said. "I believe it is your best work yet."

"Alas, a shame I cannot exhibit it in the Royal Academy of Arts, Miss Hilversham." Halsford grinned.

More guests were arriving. Rosalie and her husband were here with her newborn Nellie. Eleonore dragged

Marcus forward to introduce them. Eleonore held her granddaughter, alternately laughing and crying. She'd passed the infant on to the Duke of Rochford, who'd bounced her on his arm, somewhat disconcerted at the notion that he had a granddaughter before he had a child himself.

For Eleonore had told him earlier that day that they were expecting a child. He'd been so overcome with emotion that he'd been incapable of speaking for quite a while.

In the late afternoon, the guests dispersed to picnic, play cricket, or visit the lapidarium, a collection of ancient artefacts which Eleonore had painstakingly collected.

Eleonore looked with some wistfulness at the old house. They would move out soon, into the new building, and she felt a heaviness in her heart at the thought.

"I know I am being ridiculously maudlin," she confessed to Marcus, who'd stepped up to her. "But now that the school is finally finished, I don't want to move into it. We've been so happy here."

"Then don't," Marcus said matter-of-factly. "We stay in it."

"But Marcus. We've just furnished an entire wing in the new building, which are to be our family apartments. And the plan was that the old house is to become the boarding house for the students."

"So? Let the teachers move into the new house. They will be happy to live in brand new ducal apartments. And we stay in the rickety old wishing well house if you prefer. I don't mind either way, as long as I can be with you. It's that simple, Eleonore."

She stared at him. "It's that simple."

He pulled her up to him and placed a protective hand over her stomach and a kiss on her lips. "It is, my love. It is."

~

ABOUT THE AUTHOR

Sofi was born in Vienna, grew up in Seoul, studied Comparative Literature in Maryland, U.S.A., and lived in Quito with her Ecuadorian husband. When not writing, she likes to scramble about the countryside, exploring medieval castle ruins, which she blogs about here. She currently lives with her husband, 3 trilingual children, a sassy cat and a cheeky dog in Europe.

Get in touch and visit Sofi at her website, on Facebook or Instagram!

amazon.com/Sofi-Laporte/e/B07N1K8H6C

facebook.com/sofilaporteauthor

instagram.com/sofilaporteauthor

twitter.com/Sofi_Laporte

bookbub.com/profile/sofi-laporte